BEYOND *the* SHADOWS

ROBIN LEE HATCHER

Tyndale House Publishers, Inc.
WHEATON, ILLINOIS

Visit Tyndale's exciting Web site at www.tyndale.com

Edited by Traci DePree

Designed by Jenny Swanson

Scripture quotations are taken from the *Holy Bible,* New Living Translation, copyright © 1996. Used by permission of Tyndale House Publishers, Inc., Wheaton, Illinois 60189. All rights reserved.

This novel is a work of fiction. Names, characters, places, and incidents are either the product of the author's imagination or are used fictitiously. Any resemblance to actual events, locales, organizations, or persons living or dead is entirely coincidental and beyond the intent of either the author or publisher.

Library of Congress Cataloging-in-Publication Data

Hatcher, Robin Lee.
   Beyond the shadows : a love story / Robin Lee Hatcher.
     p. cm.
   ISBN 0-8423-5558-8
   1. Widows—Fiction.   2. Veterans—Fiction.   3. Male friendship—Fiction.   I. Title.
   PS3558.A73574B49 2004
   813'.54—dc22   2003026186

Printed in the United States of America

10   09   08   07   06   05   04
 9   8   7   6   5   4

"Robin Lee Hatcher holds nothing back in this painfully honest, deeply moving story about one couple's journey *Beyond the Shadows* of alcoholism. . . . **Beyond the Shadows has the power to change lives for good.**"

LIZ CURTIS HIGGS

BEST-SELLING AUTHOR OF *THORN IN MY HEART*

"*Beyond the Shadows* perfectly captures the raw emotions inherent in living with an alcoholic—the terrifying ambivalence between love and hatred, faith and despair. **Above all, God's mercy shines through.**"

BRANDILYN COLLINS, AUTHOR OF *BRINK OF DEATH*

"**Beautifully penned,** *Beyond the Shadows* is a testimony to the faithfulness of God and the courage of all those who dare to love . . . even when love seems futile."

ANGELA ELWELL HUNT, AUTHOR OF *THE DEBT*

"Nobody addresses modern women's issues better than Robin Lee Hatcher, and *Beyond the Shadows* is no exception."

LISA SAMSON, AUTHOR OF *THE CHURCH LADIES* AND *THE LIVING END*

"This novel honestly reveals the power of alcohol addiction and the number of innocent lives affected by it. *Beyond the Shadows* is a stark reminder of how easy it is to separate ourselves from the One who can restore us to sanity."

RICH E., GRATEFUL RECOVERING ALCOHOLIC, 9 YEARS

To Pastor Frank & Janet, to Janelle,
and to Sunni.
You loved me in the shadows
and you prayed me through to hope.

EPIGRAPH

No, no, I'm sure,

My restless spirit never could endure

To brood so long upon one luxury,

Unless it did, though fearfully, espy

A hope beyond the shadow of a dream.

John Keats, Endymion

ACKNOWLEDGMENTS

It would have been impossible to write this book without the dedication of my faithful prayer team. Every week for one full year, they lifted me, my loved ones, and this book before the throne of grace, standing in the gap with their prayers. My profound gratitude goes to: Anita C., Anna B., Arlene K., Bette B., Cathie M., Deanna K., Dianna R., Dina M., Frank M., Janelle S., Janet M., Joyce H., Kay G., Kay H., Kay M., Kay W., Kelly H., Kim K., Larna P., Lauri M., Linda H., Marion H., Melissa P., Melody P., Myra C., Norma W., Ola N., Pam K., Sharon C., and Sunni J.

Every time I think of you, I give thanks to my God. I always pray for you, and I make my requests with a heart full of joy because you have been my partners in spreading the Good News about Christ from the time you first heard it until now.

PHILIPPIANS 1:3-5

PART ONE

1955

Lead me by your truth and teach me,

for you are the God who saves me.

All day long I put my hope in you.

PSALM 25:5

March

The first time I saw him was at my husband's funeral.

It was after Pastor Clyde said his last prayer, words meant to comfort me, Andy's widow. It was after friends and people from our church and the community came and whispered their condolences as they touched my hands, which I kept folded tightly in my lap. It was after Andy's father, his face stoic in grief, led his weeping wife away. It was after my parents kissed me and told me they loved me. It was after I thought myself alone in that row of gray folding chairs at the graveside, the cold wind buffeting my back.

It was after all that when I saw him, a stranger, standing under a leafless tree, staring at the casket before it was lowered into the grave. The collar of his overcoat was turned up, and he gripped the brim of his hat with one hand, lest it be blown away. He wasn't one of those soft-spoken men from the funeral home, and he wasn't dressed like a groundskeeper. I knew he must have come because of Andy.

Seeing that I'd noticed him, he removed his hat and approached. "Mrs. Haskin." He stopped before me. "I'm sorry for your loss, ma'am."

"Thank you," I whispered, the words like sandpaper in my throat. Meaningless words, really, in a mind gone numb with pain and loss.

"Andy was a good man."

"Yes."

"The best I've ever known."

Yes.

"If there's anything I can do for you, anything you need, anything at all . . . " His sentence drifted into silence.

I nodded, wanting him to go away, wanting to be left alone. What I wanted even more was to die and go to heaven with Andy.

It wasn't right that I should be left behind. Andy and I were supposed to grow old together. Andy was supposed to build a bigger barn this summer, and I was supposed to plant roses along the white picket fence that bordered our backyard. Andy was supposed to have sons to help him on our small farm, and I was supposed to have daughters who would wear pretty ribbons in their hair and be spoiled by their daddy.

But all of that's gone now. All gone.

I stared down at my hands. Black gloves against a black skirt. Black like my heart. Black and empty and bottomless.

Oh, Andy. Andy. Why did you have to die? What will I do without you?

When I looked up again, the stranger was gone.

CHAPTER ONE

August

"Come home, Deborah," my mother had said to me countless times in the months since Andy died. "You've done your best, but it's time to be practical. It's time you sell that place and come home to live with us. Dad and I want you here. You know we do. You shouldn't be alone."

"*This* is my home, Mother," I'd always responded—words I presumed I would need to repeat often before she would be convinced I meant them.

How could I make her understand that I couldn't leave the farm? Not as long as I was able to meet the mortgage payments. This place had been Andy's dream, and letting go of it would be like letting go of him all over again. This land was all I had left of my husband, these forty acres and the small house and aging outbuildings that sat on them.

Strange, I suppose, that I wanted to stay, given it was the

farm that took Andy from me. Yet it was here, on this farm, where I felt closest to him. He'd loved the land so. He'd had the heart of a farmer beating in his chest, despite being raised in the city, despite the years he'd spent in the military, fighting wars and leading other soldiers.

It was on a hot August day, as I pondered my most recent telephone conversation with my mother, that the stranger from the cemetery came to the farm.

"Mrs. Haskin," he said from beyond the screen door, hat in hand.

"Yes?"

"I'm Gideon Clermont. I spoke to you at . . . I met you last March."

"Oh." I felt a sudden chill in my heart, as if the cold wind from that day were still buffeting me. "Yes. I remember you. We spoke at . . . at the graveside."

"Andy and I served together in Korea."

Korea. Fear had been my constant companion when Andy was in Korea. But he'd survived the war. He'd survived and come back to the States. He'd come back to me, his fiancée. I'd thought God had kept him alive so we could marry and have children and be a family. On our wedding day, Andy had promised we would grow old together.

He'd *promised* me.

Fifteen months. That was all the time we'd had as man and wife. Just fifteen months before he was taken away forever.

My legs suddenly weak, I placed my hand on the doorjamb. That's the way it always happened. One moment, I was doing all right; the next, the brokenness of my life, of my heart, stole my breath away.

"Andy saved my life," Gideon said.

Mine, too. Oh, Andy. Mine, too.

The world began to blur and slip away.

"Are you all right, Mrs. Haskin?" Gideon opened the screen door and took hold of my arm. "Here, ma'am. Let me help you inside."

I hadn't the strength to protest, so I allowed him to assist me to the nearby kitchen table, where I sank onto one of the chrome-legged chairs.

"I'll get you some water." He opened a cupboard door, closed it, then opened another, this time finding the dishware. After filling the glass at the kitchen faucet, he returned to where I sat. "You'd better drink this. You look awfully pale."

I sipped from the glass, although what I wanted most to do was return to my bed, pull the covers over my head, and wail. I wanted to scream and weep. I wanted to give up.

"Do you mind if I sit down?" Gideon asked.

I shook my head, sipped more water, then glanced at my visitor again. He was about my age, I thought, and he had thick, inky black hair, a bit disheveled from his hat, and a dark complexion. Or perhaps he'd spent a great deal of time in the sun. I couldn't be sure which. Wide-spaced brown eyes beneath dark brows watched me with gentle concern. He had a pleasant-looking mouth, and I imagined when he smiled he must be quite handsome.

I was taken by surprise by that thought. I hadn't noticed another man's looks since the day I met Andy back in 1950.

Andy . . . Oh, Andy. I miss you so much.

Gideon leaned forward on his chair. "Mrs. Haskin, I'd like to help you if I can."

"Help me?" I whispered around the lump in my throat.

"Andy was the best kind of friend. The best friend I've ever

7

had. He was like a brother to me. When I heard about his death—"
He stopped abruptly and closed his eyes, as if his words hurt him
as much as they hurt me.

It was my turn to look away. I chose to stare out the window
above the sink.

Beyond the glass I saw the barn—more of a large shed,
really—the once bright red paint now faded to a blotchy gray.
The roof sagged a little in the center.

As if reading my mind, Gideon said, "Andy wrote me last
winter and offered me a job, working with him on your farm."

"He did?" My gaze returned to the man seated across from
me. "He never mentioned it."

"He said he could use my help with building and repairs
while he did the farming." He turned his calloused hands palms-
up on the table. "I'm a carpenter by trade. I was having trouble
finding work down in California, so it seemed a good idea for
us both."

I remembered something about Gideon Clermont then.
Something Andy had written in a letter from Korea: *Gideon's
got the hands of a carpenter, and now he's come to* know *the Carpenter. Maybe that's the whole reason I was sent here, Deborah, so I could
share God's love with men who don't know Him.*

"Andy led you to Christ," I said softly. "While you were
overseas."

He smiled, a soft expression. "Yes, ma'am. He did."

"His faith was strong." I rose from my chair.

*I wish mine were as strong. O God, why can't my faith be as strong
as Andy's was?*

I walked to the sink and stared out the window at the weath-
ered barn.

You feel so far away, Lord. I need Your presence. Did You leave me when Andy died? Is that why I can't feel You near? Is that why I can't hear Your voice? Is that why I feel so utterly lost and alone?

The sound of chair legs scraping against linoleum drew me around. Gideon stood beside his chair, watching me, his smile gone. "I'd like to lend you a hand, Mrs. Haskin. I thought maybe I could come out here on weekends. You know, to do some of the things you can't do."

The things Andy would've done if he were alive.

My heart ached. I felt as if my chest were being crushed in a giant's relentless hand. "I can't afford to hire anyone, Mr. Clermont. I'm sorry. I've leased the land to a neighbor for this year, but—"

"I'm not asking you to hire me. I've got a job in Boise as a Fuller Brush salesman. It's not work I care for much, but it'll pay the rent."

"But you said Andy offered you—"

"I just want to help out, Mrs. Haskin. As Andy's friend. Will you let me help you?"

Mary Margaret Foster

I will tell you plain. I didn't much care for Gideon Clermont the first time he sauntered into our building supply and hardware store and told me he was working at the Haskin place. It just didn't seem right, him being there.

The folks of Amethyst like to take care of our own. We don't need an outsider doing it for us.

Of course, there are those who might say Deborah Haskin is herself an outsider, living here hardly more than a year. But she and Andy were active, right from the start, at Amethyst Community Church, and they both went out of their way to make friends. They didn't keep to themselves all the time, the way some newlyweds are wont to do. It's tragic, no doubt about it, what happened to her husband, and Deborah does seem mighty determined to hold on to her farm.

No, she doesn't seem like an outsider. She belongs here.

I oughta know. Me and my mister were born and raised in Amethyst. Our roots go down deep hereabouts. Our grandparents helped found this town when it was nothing but desert stolen from the jackrabbits and coyotes. We've watched the town grow since irrigation brought life to the land and prosperity to those willing to work hard for it. Before irrigation, Amethyst was just a stop on the Union Pacific Railroad and not much more. It's different now. Let me tell you.

Another thing. These are good folks who live in these parts. We don't hold with fast-living city ways. And I can tell you, the Haskins—Andy and Deborah—they fit right in after they bought the farm from old Mr. Smythe.

Andy Haskin had a real fire in his belly for farming, but talk about a greenhorn! Still, he was willing to learn. The Bible says if you get all the advice and instruction you can, you'll be wise for the rest of your life, so I figured Andy was going to be plenty wise. He was like a sponge, soaking up advice from other farmers, always asking questions of everybody he met. I couldn't count the times he did that, right here in our store.

Well, I'll tell you, it was a shame, the accident that took his life. A real tragedy.

Deborah Haskin was tore up inside. You could see it in her eyes, even when she put a brave smile on her lips.

Yes, indeedy. It was a tragedy what happened to that young couple. A real tragedy.

And now there was that Clermont fellow—smiling, handsome, mighty sure of himself—from California, he told me, saying he was making repairs and doing odd jobs at the Haskin farm. He claimed to be a friend of Andy's. But I ask you, what did Deborah know about him? What did any of us know about him?

No; like I said before, I didn't care much for Gideon Clermont when I first met him. Not one bit.

CHAPTER TWO

I was washing my breakfast dishes when Gideon drove into the yard and backed up his Ford close to the barn. He cut the engine and got out of the truck—a vehicle as faded as the structure behind it.

Heidi, my one-year-old collie, left the shade of the porch and ran to Gideon, her tail wagging. The dog had taken to him from the start—but then, Heidi loved everybody. A watchdog she wasn't.

Gideon spoke to Heidi and gave her head a few pats; then he strode to the rear of the pickup, dropped the tailgate, rolled up his shirtsleeves, and began to unload the shingles he'd purchased at the building supply store in Amethyst. He was a hard worker. He'd proven that on the past two Saturdays. It was amazing how much he'd accomplished in so short a time, not to mention how little money he'd spent to get the work done.

The shingles for the barn roof, however, couldn't be had on the cheap. I had told Gideon to charge them to my account, but while he was still in the store, Mrs. Foster had called to confirm it was all right. I imagined she thought him some sort of charlatan.

I crossed the kitchen to the back door, pushed open the screen, and called, "Would you like some coffee?"

He laid a bundle of shingles next to a growing pile alongside the barn before answering me. "No thanks, Mrs. Haskin. I had plenty before I drove out this morning."

I stepped onto the porch, allowing the screen door to swing closed behind me. "Are you sure? It wouldn't be any trouble. It's already made."

"I'm sure, ma'am, but thanks for the offer." He went back to work.

For some reason, the solitude of the house seemed depressing. Rather than return to it, I walked toward Gideon and the pickup truck.

"You're making me feel as old as my mother," I said as I drew near. "Maybe it's time you called me Deborah instead of *ma'am*."

He stopped again. "I'd like that." His grin broadened. "And I'm Gideon."

It bothered me a little, how much I liked his smile.

With a mischievous glint in his eye, he asked, "How old *are* you, anyway? And how old's your mother?"

"None of your business, *Mr.* Clermont." My answer was tart, but there wasn't any sting in the words. My grin took care of that.

Gideon grabbed another bundle of shingles. "You didn't ask, but in case you're curious, I'm thirty." His biceps bulged as he lifted the load and turned away.

"Have you always lived in California?"

"I was born there, in Riverside." He set down the shingles and faced me again. "Lived there all my life."

It felt good to have someone to talk to, and I didn't want to return to the solitude of the house. Not just yet. "And your family? Do you have brothers or sisters?"

"I have two older brothers, both married. Jack's four years older than me. He's the father of three, one boy and two girls. My other brother, Bob, is three years older than me. He's got three kids, too. Two boys, one girl." He grinned as he walked back to the truck. "Makes for quite a mob at our family get-togethers, I'll tell you."

"I always wanted to be part of a large family." The words slipped out before I knew they'd formed.

Gideon wiped sweat from his brow with his forearm. "No siblings?"

"No. Just me."

"Can't imagine what that's like. When we were kids, my brothers and I shared a bedroom. We did just about everything together. Course, I was the youngest so I wasn't always welcome when I tagged along. But Mom made Jack and Bob put up with me."

"Do you see your brothers often?"

"Yeah. Pretty often. They both live within half an hour of the house where we grew up. My folks love that 'cause they can see their grandkids a lot." He put one foot on the tailgate of the truck, then rested his forearms on his raised thigh. "What about you, Deborah? Where'd you grow up?"

"In Boise." I leaned against the side of the pickup. "My parents still live there." I sighed softly, remembering my mother's latest plea for me to sell the farm and move home.

Why couldn't she understand that *this* was my home? "I'm thirty-one, for pity's sake."

Laughter burst from Gideon, undoubtedly more because of my horrified expression—I hadn't *meant* to speak my thoughts aloud—than what I'd actually said. After my surprise had a chance to wear off, I began to laugh, too.

Oh, my. I hadn't laughed in such a long time.

And so I laughed . . .

And laughed . . .

Until I cried.

Gideon had the good graces to keep his distance. He didn't try to pat my shoulder and murmur any of those good-intentioned but clichéd words of comfort people so often said. He simply stood there and waited until I cried myself out. Then he handed me a handkerchief, saying, "It's clean."

"Thank you." I dried my eyes.

"Not a problem."

I blew my nose.

"You're entitled, you know."

I looked up to see that there were tears swimming before his dark eyes.

I'm not sure, but I think that was the moment I began to fall for Gideon—because we both loved and missed Andy.

I wonder how many people would think that strange.

— *Merle Johnson* —

My wife, Gertrude, and me, we own the dairy farm across the road and down a piece from the old Smythe place. We were glad when the Haskins came along and bought it before it went to rot and ruin, standing empty the way it had for so long.

They were sweet on each other, those two. Married just a few months, him out of the army not much longer than that. Every time we'd see the two of them together, Gertrude would elbow me in the ribs and say something like, "Remember what it was like, Merle, to be young and in love like them?"

Sure I do. You'd think she'd know that, living with me like she has for near on thirty years. Love's what got us through the lean times—and there was more than a few of those, that's for sure.

I was there the day Andy Haskin died. Well, I didn't see it happen, but I was the one who come running when I heard Deborah screaming for help.

Mercy, it was a scene straight out of a nightmare, that tractor turned over on top of Andy, blood coming out of his mouth and his eyes open but not seeing. Deborah, she was pushing on that big old machine like she thought she could lift it off him and bring him back to life. I guess she couldn't see it was already too late by then.

They say there's a time to be born and a time to die, but I have a hard time believing it was time for Andy Haskin to leave this good earth. Some things it's just hard for a body to understand. This was one of those things.

Gertrude and me, we did what we could to help Deborah through the worst of those first weeks after the accident. Turns out she got some money from a life insurance policy Andy carried, and I got her a fair lease price from Tom Dailey, her neighbor to the north. He's growing alfalfa on the Haskin forty acres this summer and doing all right for himself. He would've cheated her if he could have and never paid no mind to her being a widow. The old Scrooge. Tom's got his good points, but he can squeeze a dollar till the eagle starts losing feathers.

We didn't know Deborah Haskin hired herself a handyman to help around the place until he'd already been working there a couple of weeks. Just Saturdays, according to Mary Margaret Foster at the hardware store. When Mary Margaret called, she gave Gertrude a list of everything the man bought and put on Deborah's account.

When I heard the fellow was a stranger to the area, I decided I'd best hoof it over and have a look-see for myself. But by then he'd left for the day. Deborah told me the man—Gideon Clermont by name—was an army buddy of Andy's.

I admit. That made me willing to give him the benefit of the doubt. I served in Europe during the First World War, and I know how those strong bonds form between soldiers. If Gideon was a friend of Andy's *and* a veteran, I figured he was all right.

Still, I meant to make his acquaintance, just as soon as I could.

CHAPTER THREE

From the very first, I've loved twilight on the farm. I think the world turns a bit more slowly in the gloaming than it does at other hours, especially in the country.

On that August evening, I stood on the back porch, my arms wrapped around the post near the steps, and watched the lengthening shadows. Crickets chirped a continuous chorus. The lowing of cows could be heard from the neighbor's farm, and the sweet scent of alfalfa filled the cooling night air. The branches of the trees that formed the border with Tom Dailey's farm danced and swayed as restless birds flitted from one branch to the next.

Ah, yes. I loved twilight on the farm.

The last rays of sunlight kissed the roof of the barn, a roof that no longer sagged, a roof that wouldn't leak when the autumn rains came. Gideon had proven himself as good as his word.

I pushed away from the post and left the porch. Heidi appeared beside me, trotting in that ladylike manner of hers. Glad for her company, I gave her head a few pats of welcome without breaking stride.

We strolled past the barn, past the corral, past the chicken coop and the vegetable garden and the haystack. We walked straight into the field of alfalfa, tall and green as time for the third cutting grew closer. The evening sounds softened as stars began to twinkle overhead.

I stopped, closed my eyes, and listened.

I suppose I hoped to hear something from God. I suppose I hoped He would tell me at last why I was alive and Andy was in heaven, why all of my plans had been dashed in an afternoon. Certainly I'd asked Him the question often enough in the past five months. Sometimes I hadn't asked. Sometimes I'd demanded. But neither asking nor demanding had brought me an answer.

In truth, the only answer I wanted was to look up and find Andy there.

"I thought it was going to be different, Heidi." I sighed and looked at the stars again. Louder this time, I said, "Why isn't it different?"

The song of the night was my only reply.

I walked back toward the house, memories churning.

I was a senior in high school when the Japanese attacked Pearl Harbor, a Sunday morning no one who was alive then would ever forget. The following summer, at the age of eighteen, I went to work as a secretary at Gowen Field, where so many young men were stationed during the war years. That was where I first met Andy Haskin. Years later, when we met again, he pretended he remembered meeting me there, but I knew he didn't. Andy was a pathetic liar. Never the least bit believable when he stretched the truth.

Oh, Andy. I miss you so. I miss your pitiful attempts to pull the wool over my eyes. I miss your teasing. I miss your lazy smile and the goodness of your heart. I miss seeing you toss the ball for Heidi. I miss hearing you sing hymns beside me in church. I miss you. I miss you. I miss you.

Reaching the porch, I sank onto the bottom step. Heidi lay beside me, placed her head on my thigh, and stared up at me, her eyes black pools in the light from the kitchen.

"You always read my mood. Don't you, girl? You know I'm thinking of Andy."

My parents had despaired over me. They'd thought I would never meet a man and settle down, the way their friends' daughters were doing. It wasn't as if I hadn't dated plenty of guys, but none of them had been *the* guy.

Until Andy.

I groaned.

I wanted to scream.

"Come on, Heidi. Let's go to bed."

I rose and went inside, my collie following close behind, her nails *clip-clipping* on the floor.

It didn't take long to lock the house and turn off the lights; only a little longer than that to wash my face, brush my teeth, and slip into my nightgown. Heidi curled onto her side on the rag rug at the foot of my bed while I pushed aside the top sheet and bedspread and lay on my back, waiting for sleep to come.

The bed felt too big with only one in it.

I rolled onto my belly and pressed my face into my pillow, wondering if it was possible to smother myself by simply lying very still. Would lack of oxygen cause me to lose consciousness, followed by a painless death? Perhaps no one would find me for days and days.

But I didn't lie still. Instead, I curled onto my side and wrapped my arms around my pillow the way I used to wrap my arms around my husband. Tears—those hated betrayers of my feelings—dampened the pillowcase.

"Make it stop, God," I whispered. "I don't want to feel like this anymore. Make it stop."

Pastor Clyde Beekman

It's especially difficult for me when I see one of my flock pulling away from God. Deborah Haskin was a good case in point.

The first thing the Haskins did after they moved to their farm was come into town to make my acquaintance. In love with each other and in love with the Lord, they settled into the life of our small church, and before you knew it, it seemed they'd been members all their lives.

Andy Haskin was soon leading the adult Sunday school class. He was a gifted teacher, and I was thankful to have him. More than once I wondered if he'd missed his calling, if that calling wasn't to the farm but to the pulpit. What I admired most about Andy was his hunger to know God more and more, and that hunger spilled onto all the people who knew him, making them hungry, too.

But it was Deborah I wanted to tell you about. Deborah has a gift of her own, a wonderful ability to draw people outside themselves, especially teenage girls. I had every expectation of seeing her lead our youth one day, but that expectation dimmed with Andy's death. I thought it would be a temporary delay. I hoped it would, even as I saw Deborah withdrawing from the fellowship of the saints. She sat stiffly in the pew on Sundays, and she stopped singing the hymns altogether.

My heart told me Deborah was using her sorrow to build a wall between herself and her Master. She didn't stop attending church, though there were occasional absences. Nor did she outwardly deny her faith in Christ, for she still believed in Him. I knew that. But I suspected her belief was now without the assurance of Christ's unconditional love for her.

I grieved for what was happening within Deborah, but my words of comfort and counsel fell on deaf ears.

CHAPTER FOUR

September. Warm days. Cool nights. Frosty mornings. Scents that promised the coming of harvest.

As I left the house that Friday morning, the crisp air made me draw down into my coat like a turtle pulling into its shell. Come this afternoon, I knew I would be wearing shorts while I worked in the garden.

And work in the garden I must. If I didn't get the tomatoes off the vines, one of these mornings I would find them damaged by frost.

Mother was coming to the farm that afternoon, even though I'd tried to convince her to wait a few days. "Why don't you come on Monday, Mother? I'll have the tomatoes picked and ready for canning. We'll put up some of your spaghetti sauce and have a nice visit at the same time."

"I couldn't possibly come on Monday, dear. I play bridge with the girls."

"Oh, yes. I forgot."

"Well, I hope you haven't forgotten your father's birthday, too. It's right around the corner, and we'll expect you to be with us for supper."

"No, Mother. I haven't forgotten Dad's birthday. I'll be there."

"Good. Well, I'll see you Friday, dear. Good-bye."

Why was it, I wondered now, that my mother so often made me feel like a disobedient child?

The horses in the corral nickered softly as I approached. Daniel and Boone, we'd named the dun geldings, because Andy had said their coloring reminded him of coonskin caps. I stopped to stroke their muzzles and give them sugar cubes from my pocket. Then I opened the gate to turn them out to pasture.

The crunch of tires on gravel drew me around, and I was surprised to see Gideon's pickup pulling up to the barn. Heidi trotted over to welcome him. I followed at a more sedate pace.

"Morning," Gideon said as he got out of the cab.

"Good morning. I . . . I wasn't expecting you today."

"I picked up a carpentry job that I start tomorrow." He shrugged. "I covered extra territory yesterday in my sales route to free up today." He jerked his head toward the corral. "That fence needs work before the bad weather sets in, or your horses are going to be loose some night. I didn't want to put it off another week."

He was right. The fence did need work. There were a lot of things that still needed attention before bad weather set in, more than I cared to think about.

But fewer than before, thanks to Gideon.

He strapped on his tool belt and started to turn away.

"I've got coffee on the stove," I said. "Want some?"

I always asked. He always declined.

I'd already taken a step toward the coop, certain of his answer—and was startled when he said, "Sure. Thanks."

I halted.

"Feed the chickens first," he said, amusement evident in his voice. "Then get the coffee?"

"Ah . . . yes."

"I'll give you a hand."

In the weeks Gideon had been coming to the farm, making his repairs, working his magic in countless ways, we'd spent only brief moments together. I was grateful he wasn't the pushy sort, wanting to talk when I didn't feel like it. I couldn't have tolerated that.

It occurred to me, as the two of us spread the feed to the clucking poultry, that my neighbor Merle Johnson most likely knew more about Gideon than I did. Merle had dropped by on two separate Saturdays to visit with my "handyman," as he referred to Gideon. I suspect those talks were more interviews than friendly chats. Gideon must have passed muster. Otherwise, Merle would have spoken to me about him.

I cast a sideways glance in Gideon's direction. After all Gideon had done for me in these weeks, it must seem to him that I'd shown little gratitude. I resolved to change that. I would be more friendly. I would show a little interest in him as a fellow human being. That was the least I could do.

A short while later, we were inside the house, Gideon seated at the kitchen table while I filled two large cups with hot coffee.

"How do you take it?" I asked.

"Black, thanks."

I carried his cup to the table and set it before him, then returned to the counter where I added a splash of fresh cream and a spoonful of sugar to my coffee. "So . . . " I turned around, cup held in both hands, and leaned my backside against the counter. "You begin a carpentry job tomorrow?"

He nodded. "That's right. A temporary one. A day's worth of work at most."

"In Boise?"

He nodded again.

"I'm sure they'll be glad they hired you."

"I hope so." He took a drink of his coffee. "I'd like to hire on permanently with the construction firm." With a slow shake of his head, he added, "I'm not much of a salesman. I like meeting people all right, but convincing them to buy products they may not want or need isn't up my alley."

"Andy said you—" As quick as that, my throat grew tight, and I couldn't say anything more.

After a long, uncomfortable silence, Gideon said, "Did I tell you I just became an uncle again?" I knew he was changing the subject on purpose, to give me time to collect myself. "Night before last. My brother Jack's newest addition."

I blinked, swallowed, then managed, "No, you didn't mention it." I feigned a smile.

"A nephew. Nine pounds, four ounces. They named him Frankie. My sister-in-law is gaga over Sinatra."

The ache in my chest eased a bit, and my smile grew more genuine.

"Now it's four boys to three girls." Gideon slid his coffee cup back from the edge of the table. "Maybe I'll get to tip the odds the other direction when I start a family."

"Are you getting married?"

"Me?" He laughed. "Not any time soon. I've got to find someone who likes me first."

"That shouldn't be a problem." Heat flared in my cheeks the instant the words were out of my mouth. I sounded as though I was flirting, for Pete's sake!

Once again, he was gracious. "Thanks. It isn't easy to meet women. Not the sort of women I'm interested in meeting anyway."

I was curious to know what sort that would be, but I resisted the urge to ask as I moved to the table and sat opposite Gideon.

"I'd like to meet someone who enjoys simple pleasures." He gave his shoulders a slight shrug. "I'd like to find someone to grow old with."

Andy and I planned to grow old together.

The look in his eyes suggested he'd read my thoughts.

"What else?" I asked, despite the sudden tightness in my throat.

"Well, a Christian woman, of course. It's important to share the same beliefs."

"Yes." I ran the tip of my index finger around the rim of my coffee cup. "That is important."

I thought again of Andy. I'd loved sitting beside him in church, the two of us holding hands beneath our open Bible. I'd loved saying our evening prayers together. I'd felt so safe, so secure, because of him.

These days, my Bible lay unopened on my nightstand. I had no one to pray with and so prayers went unspoken. Nothing felt safe and secure anymore.

If only Andy hadn't been careless when driving that tractor. If only the machine hadn't tipped over when the wheel dropped into the ditch. If only I'd gone with him that morning. If only . . .

We'd been so happy. We'd done all the things we were supposed to do—worked hard, gone to church, prayed together, cared for each other. We'd lived our lives by the rules.

And still Andy had died.

Gideon said, "I'd better get to that fence."

I didn't say anything to stop his going. I was too lost in my grief.

———

It was nearly noon when my mother's dark green Nash turned into the drive. I was in the garden, filling a bushel basket with ripe tomatoes. Gideon was hammering a new top rail onto a fence post.

"Who is that young man, Deborah?" Mother asked as soon as she and I reached the back porch, my arms wrapped around the basket of tomatoes.

"A friend of Andy's. He's helping make a few repairs around the farm."

"Oh."

There was a world of disapproval in that tiny word. It said her widowed, thirty-one-year-old daughter should not be living alone in the country. It said her daughter should not have a good-looking, unattached man working there without proper supervision. It asked, *What will the bridge ladies think of this?*

"I've invited Evelyn Yost and her son Fred to join us for your father's birthday dinner."

I loved my mother with my whole heart. Really and truly. But sometimes she did tend to meddle.

"You remember Fred, don't you, dear?"

"Yes, Mother. I remember him."

Fred Yost, who combed those three dozen strands of hair

over his shiny pate, hoping no one would notice he was bald. That Fred Yost.

Oh, Mother. How could you think it?

I glanced toward the corral, where Gideon was nailing another rail to a post. "I hope you won't mind, but I've asked—" I nearly choked on the lie— "Mr. Clermont to join us, too."

"You what?"

"I've asked Gideon to come with me to Dad's birthday dinner." The falsehood came a little easier this time, in a rush now. "He doesn't know very many people because he only moved to Idaho last spring. I thought it would be the right thing to do, asking him to come with me. He was a *very* good friend of Andy's."

"Deborah . . . I—"

"Wait here, Mother. I'll bring him over to introduce you." I dashed away before she had a chance to stop me.

Oh, please don't be busy. Please don't think I'm awful. Please rescue me from Fred Yost.

Gideon saw me coming. He paused in his labors, then pulled a kerchief from his back pocket and wiped the sweat from his forehead.

"I need your help," I said softly as I stopped before him.

"Sure." His gaze flicked over my shoulder, then returned to me. "What do you need?"

"That's my mother. I told her I was bringing you to my father's birthday dinner next Friday."

He raised an eyebrow.

"She's trying to set me up with the son of a friend."

The hint of a smile lifted the corners of his mouth. "Ah. I'm the decoy."

"Gideon, I—"

"It's okay. I've got a mom, too." He rolled his eyes. "I'm thirty and unmarried, and my mother's got lots of friends and acquaintances with daughters."

"Then you won't mind coming?"

"Of course I won't mind. What else are friends for?" His grin broadened, and there was a mischievous twinkle in his eyes. "I kind of like being the knight on a white horse riding to the rescue."

— *Bernice Richardson* —

I want nothing more than my daughter's happiness. Although she grew up and left home years ago, Deborah is *still* a child in my heart. My only child. I can't help wanting to protect her, to shield her from the harsh realities of life. It doesn't matter in the least that I know I can't shield her forever. I still want to try.

It's absolute foolishness that has kept my daughter on that farm. I didn't think it particularly wise when she and Andy bought the place. Neither of them knew anything about farming. But I managed to hold my tongue back then, and I must confess, they did appear blissfully happy.

But the accident that took Andy's life changed everything. I thought Deborah would act prudently and return to the city. She's an experienced secretary. She could find suitable employment. She could work with interesting people until she met a man and got married again. She wants children. Time is slipping away. She shouldn't waste it on that farm. She's secluded herself in the past few months. That isn't healthy. She rarely drives into Boise to see her father and me or to shop. I'm the one who usually picks up the telephone to call her. When I do, she's disinterested in the things I have to tell her.

I haven't expected Deborah's grief to pass quickly. It's only been six months. I know it takes time to recover from the loss of one's husband. But I don't want Deborah to stop living, either. This may sound harsh, but it was Andy who died. Not Deborah. She needs to remember that.

I could tell my daughter expected me to disapprove of Gideon Clermont. To tell you the truth, I thought I would, too, but I didn't. The moment she brought him over to the front porch and introduced us that Friday in September, I liked him—and I'm a good judge of character, or so I've been told. For one thing, he had the most charming smile. For another, he had a firm handshake. I like that in a person and most of all in a man. Gideon looked me straight in the eyes. That's an important sign of character and integrity.

But most of all, I saw the way Gideon looked at Deborah, and I suspected he was smitten with her. That alone would have caused me to feel fondly toward him. I wanted my daughter's happiness above all things. I couldn't say at the time if this man would make her happy or if he was meant to be part of her future, but at least he might be a step in the right direction.

CHAPTER FIVE

I told Gideon I would meet him at my parents' home. There was no need for him to drive all the way out to the farm only to turn around and drive back to Boise for dinner. That's what I told him, but he wouldn't hear of it.

"If I'm going to play a knight to the rescue," he said, "I'm going to do it right."

The day of my father's birthday was one of those warm Indian-summer days that we are blessed with in southern Idaho. Cool nights had brushed the tree leaves with hints of yellow and orange, and the fire bushes that bordered Gertrude Johnson's front yard were the most brilliant shade of red I'd ever seen. A haze lingered over the land, the earth stirred up by the harvesters, a haze turned gold by the waning sun.

I heard Gideon's truck approaching moments before I could see it. Strange, the way I'd become attuned to that particular sound after only a few weeks. I reached for my sweater and pocketbook, then stepped onto the back porch as Gideon brought the pickup to a halt. Through the cab's front window, I saw him wave. More of a salute, actually. I waved back.

"Sorry I'm late," he said as he disembarked.

I checked my wristwatch. "You're not late. You're right on time."

"Am I?" He rested one foot on the bottom step. "You look very pretty tonight, Deborah Haskin."

Silly though it was, heat rose up my neck and into my cheeks. "Thank you."

I didn't tell him, but he looked nice too. He'd dressed in a suit and tie, and his dark hair was slicked back. Freshly showered, I suspected, after a day of work.

Gideon offered a hand to assist me down the steps. "Your white horse awaits."

He's a romantic, I thought. The discovery made me smile.

I took his hand, and he escorted me to the truck, opening the door for me, holding my elbow as I stepped into the cab, making sure I was settled before he closed the door again.

It seemed forever and a day since I'd been treated with such tenderness. Not that my family, friends, and neighbors hadn't done their best to care for me in my period of mourning. But this was something different, this special way a man treats a woman. This was the way Andy had treated me—the same, yet different, too.

For Andy had been Andy.

And Gideon was Gideon.

We didn't talk a lot during the drive into Boise. His truck engine was noisy, and the springs were nearly nonexistent. At one point, over a particularly rough stretch of gravel road,

Gideon glanced at me, saw my death grip on the armrest and the pained expression on my face, and began to laugh. He didn't have to say why.

I laughed, too.

In that moment, I felt peace flow through me. For that moment, I wasn't afraid for my future and I wasn't overwhelmed by my grief. I felt a tiny spark of hope, a hope that one day I would know happiness again.

I wasn't happy yet, but I had hope.

———

While the men—Dad, Gideon, and Fred Yost—swapped war stories in the living room, the ladies gathered in the kitchen, my mother busy with last-minute preparations.

"How did you meet him?" Evelyn Yost asked in a stage whisper.

"Gideon? He was a friend of Andy's. They served together in Korea."

I wondered how many times in the future I would be asked that question and have to repeat my answer. Then I wondered why I would wonder it. I couldn't expect Gideon to give me his Saturdays forever. Nor could I expect him to be my knight on a white horse—that thought brought a smile—rescuing me from those who wanted to introduce me to the unmarried sons of their friends or to their brothers or to their third cousins thrice removed. Eventually there would come a time when Gideon would take another job that didn't give him Saturdays off or he would move away or he would find a woman to love and to marry.

Those thoughts took my smile away.

Evelyn said something to Mother, but I no longer listened.

I turned toward the kitchen doorway and looked through it to the living room where the men were seated, Gideon beside my father on the sofa and Fred in a nearby chair.

I didn't want Gideon to take another job . . .

Or move away . . .

Or find a woman to love and marry.

It was confusing to feel this way, to think this way. How was it possible to miss my husband with such ferocity and yet want—

I closed my eyes. *Want what? What is it I want?*

"Deborah," Mother said, "please tell the men that dinner is ready."

Glad for the interruption, I shoved my confusion into a dark corner of my mind and went to do my mother's bidding.

In short order, we were all seated around the dining-room table, Dad at the head, Mother at the foot. Gideon sat at my father's left hand with me beside him. The Yosts were opposite us.

I had always loved our family dinners. Despite my wish for a sibling or two, my childhood had been one of happiness and laughter. Oh, I could get frustrated that Mother sometimes forgot I was a grown woman now, but I knew she acted out of love and the goodness of her heart. And Dad? Well, I was the apple of his eye.

Andy had fit right into our family. He and Dad had been thick as thieves. They loved to argue, good-naturedly, about which sports teams were the best. Mom had adored him, too. She—

"Thanks for asking me to bring you, Deb," Gideon said softly. "I like your folks."

I met his gaze. There was an odd fluttering sensation in my chest, and I knew I wanted Gideon in my life even as I remembered and missed Andy.

It seemed wrong for me to feel that way.

Was it?

Gideon smiled, a teasing twinkle in his eyes, and I realized I'd been staring at him without acknowledging his comment. A blush rose in my cheeks—the second time tonight—and that made me feel even more embarrassed.

"Well," my father said, "let's bless this food, shall we? So we can eat."

Once again, I was thankful for an interruption, a reason to look away from Gideon, to close my eyes and clear my thoughts.

— *Henry Richardson* —

Bernice thought our daughter needed a husband, the sooner the better. Of course, my wife also thought we needed grandchildren, the sooner the better.

Gotta love that woman, for all her interfering ways.

I remember that Friday she rushed home to tell me about this Clermont fellow who was working on the farm. "Henry, I believe he's in love with Deborah," she said.

I wasn't so sure that was good news, but Bernice seemed to think so.

The past six months were hard ones for my family. I've never known a better man than my son-in-law. Oh, sometimes I thought Andy was a little too religious, but at least he lived it. There wasn't anything fake about him. Losing Andy was rough on all of us but, of course, hardest of all on my daughter. Watching Deborah suffer, that near ripped my heart right out of my chest. A man ought never have to see his child suffer like that. It isn't right. It isn't the proper order of things.

So seeing Deborah smiling as we sat around the dinner table was like a fresh breeze blowing through the house.

If Gideon Clermont was the one who put it there, her smile, then I was all for him.

CHAPTER SIX

Stars twinkled in a moonless sky, and when Gideon cut the truck's engine outside my house, the sudden silence and darkness of night seemed all-enveloping. I found myself holding my breath, waiting . . . for something.

"Thanks, Deborah."

I glanced toward Gideon, and though I couldn't see him well, I knew he was looking at me.

"I had a great time tonight. I've missed this kind of family get-together since moving to Idaho. Your folks are terrific."

I smiled, warmed by his words.

"I hope . . . Well, I hope they liked me, too."

"They did."

He cleared his throat. "That's important to me."

Again, I held my breath. It seemed a long while before I asked, "Why?"

"Because you're important to me."

He leaned toward me, and by instinct, I leaned toward him, too.

Our first kiss . . .

It was tentative . . .

I felt tempted.

It was tender . . .

I felt treasured.

It was turbulent . . .

I felt treasonous.

"I know," Gideon whispered as our lips parted.

"You know what?"

"You're wondering what right we have to . . . to do this? To be with each other. To kiss. We wouldn't have the right if Andy were still alive."

He placed the palm of his left hand on my right cheek. I closed my eyes and leaned into it. I felt the warmth of his body, so close to my own. The faint scent of his cologne tickled my nostrils. I swear I could hear the beating of our hearts in unison.

Warm tears slipped from beneath my eyelids.

Gideon leaned forward again and kissed the tears away, then said, "You have a right to live, Deb. Both of us do. We loved Andy, but he's gone and we're still here." He paused, then asked, "Don't you think he'd want you to find happiness if there's a chance for it?"

"I don't know what he'd want." I reached for the truck door and opened it. "I don't know."

"Yes, you do." Gideon's hands on my shoulders stayed my flight. "Andy loved you more than life itself. He talked about you all the time when we were in Korea. He wanted you to be happy. Before his own happiness, he wanted yours. You know that about him. He wouldn't want you to feel guilty for being alive."

"Stop, Gideon. Please stop. Don't say any more."

"Look. I don't know what'll happen between us. Maybe nothing. Maybe something great." His fingers tightened their hold on me. "I came to Idaho to work for a good friend. I stayed because I wanted to help his widow get through a bad time. I never expected it to be anything more than that. But there's something happening between the two of us, and I want to find out what it is. Don't you?"

He's right. I feel guilty. I feel guilty for being alive. I feel guilty because I can feel. I can feel because I'm alive. I can feel! But Andy can't. Andy will never feel anything ever again.

I lowered my chin toward my chest.

If I really loved Andy—if I still love him the way I thought I did— how could I let Gideon kiss me like that? How can I want him to take me back in his arms and kiss me again?

"I'm not asking for any promises." Gideon's voice was low, deep, emotional. "I know it's too soon. I'm only asking for a chance. Will you give us a chance, Deb?"

A heartbeat . . .

Two . . .

Five . . .

Ten . . .

"Yes," I answered. *I'm sorry, Andy. I'm so sorry.* "Yes, I'll give us a chance."

I heard Gideon release a breath; then his hands slipped from my shoulders even as he leaned forward to brush his lips against my cheek. "I'll see you to the door."

Our parting on the back porch was both quick and awkward. He didn't try to embrace or kiss me again, and I wasn't sure if I was sorry or glad for that. Once we'd said good night and I was inside the house, I leaned my back against the kitchen door, not bothering to switch on the light. I waited, breathlessly, to hear Gideon start the truck and drive away. It seemed forever before he did.

Finally, when the silence of night had encompassed me again, I pushed away from the door and made my way to the bedroom. I undressed in the dark, slipped my nightgown over my head, and crawled into bed, not bothering to brush my teeth or wash my face. It seemed too much effort.

I don't know what I'm doing, God. I don't know the answers to . . . to anything. I don't know what I'm supposed to do or supposed to feel. I feel confused and guilty and angry and afraid and lonely and sad. I loved Andy so much, and he's gone. And now there's Gideon . . . Where are You, God? Why don't You answer me? Don't You care that I'm hurting and confused? Are You even there?

— *Gertrude Johnson* —

My friends will tell you I'm not one to gossip. When I hear something in confidence, I don't repeat it. Not a word. But bless my soul, I confess it was hard not to tell the ladies in my church circle about that telephone call.

It was on a Monday evening. I remember distinctly which night it was because *The George Burns and Gracie Allen Show* had just ended. That's my favorite television program. It was a very funny episode where George, Gracie, and their friends the Mortons travel by train to New York City. I was wiping tears of laughter from my eyes when the telephone rang. Of course, I should have realized it wasn't *our* ring, but I suppose I was only listening with one ear.

Anyway, I lifted the receiver and was about to say, "Hello," when I heard a man's voice on the other end of the line and then I heard Deborah Haskin reply. I should have put the receiver down immediately. Everyone on a party line knows the proper protocol. But once I'd hesitated . . .

Well, what would *you* have done? I ask you that. Especially if you heard, as I did, Gideon Clermont asking Deborah out to dinner and the movies.

And glory be! She said yes.

I don't think Merle was the least bit surprised when I told him. Oh, I know I said I don't gossip, but telling my husband isn't the same thing. Merle and I, we've got no secrets from each other, not after all the years we've been married. One look at my face would've told him I knew something he didn't, and he would have made me tell.

I wish Mary Margaret over at the hardware store was as good at worming things out of me so I could have told her, too. I thought I'd burst from holding in that juicy little secret.

CHAPTER SEVEN

The guilt I felt for being alive and able to care for another man didn't go away immediately, but after the night of Dad's birthday dinner, it did begin to fade.

Gideon, ever the gentleman, let me work through my emotions without interference. He showed up to work at my place for the next three Saturdays and was warm and cordial, but he didn't push me. He seemed to know what I needed, sometimes before I knew it myself. To be honest, by the time he got around to asking me out, I was feeling more than a little impatient.

Did he know that, too?

When Gideon came for me that Friday evening in October, I was as nervous as a teenager going on her first date. I'd changed my dress three different times. Was this one too dressy? Was that one too casual? Did this one make me look too matronly? Did that one make me look chunky? Finally, I settled on a full skirt of robin's-egg blue and a sleeveless white bodice.

Gideon's expressive brown eyes told me I'd chosen the right outfit the instant I opened the door for him.

"Hi," he said.

"Hi." My heart did a funny little pitter-pat.

"You look pretty."

He'd told me that before, and like the last time, I blushed. I felt giddy and oh-so-foolish at the same time.

"I like your hair like that."

My mind went blank. I couldn't remember what I'd done with my hair. I had to lift a hand and feel it. Oh, yes. I'd skipped my usual ponytail. My hair was baby fine and impossible to do much of anything with. I almost never left it down around my shoulders.

"Are you ready?" Gideon asked.

I nodded. "Yes." I grabbed my sweater and draped it over my shoulders. "I'm ready."

Minutes later, Gideon turned out of the driveway and headed toward Amethyst.

As if sensing my surprise that we weren't going to Boise, he said, "They're playing *Mister Roberts* at the Rialto. I've heard it's a great movie. You haven't seen it yet, have you?"

"No." I hadn't been to the movies in a year.

"Merle tells me the food at Julia's Café is good, so I thought we'd eat dinner there. I hope you're not disappointed we're staying in Amethyst."

I had one of those flashes of understanding, the kind where a person *knows* something for no apparent reason. Gideon wanted us to be seen together. He wanted my friends and neighbors to know he was staking his claim.

I imagined us as Tarzan and Jane. Or should that be Alley Oop and Ooola?

I swallowed a laugh as I turned to look out the window, relaxed and inexplicably happy.

Julia's Café was Amethyst's one and only eatery. The decor—and the menu—had changed little since the restaurant opened in 1905. It remained the same favored gathering place today that it was in the early part of the century.

The dining room was nearly full when Gideon and I entered at half past six. Slowly, heads raised and turned, and conversations dwindled until the only sounds came from the kitchen at the back of the restaurant.

For the second time in less than an hour, I blushed, which made me feel even more conspicuous. But Gideon didn't seem bothered in the least. He nodded and half grinned at the craning heads, as if people always fell silent when he entered a room.

Alice Gordon, the gum-popping, full-figured waitress who worked most Friday nights, grabbed two tattered menus from the end of the lunch counter. "This way," she said in that bored-sounding voice of hers, then led the way to a table in the far corner of the café.

It was amazing the way everyone was able to watch our progress, yet not make eye contact with me. Vera Beekman and Mary Margaret Foster were both smiling at their plates; you'd have thought the food had said something amusing by the looks on their faces. Gertrude Johnson leaned across the table to whisper something to Merle, who then shook his head.

"Here you go." Alice dropped the menus onto the plastic red-and-white-checkered tablecloth. "I'll be back in a bit to take your order."

"Thanks." Gideon pulled out the nearest chair for me, and as I sat down, he softly said, "Don't worry. They'll forget about us in a minute or two."

I hoped he was right—and he was. Little by little, conversations resumed until the restaurant was buzzing as noisily as when we'd entered.

"See?" Seated across from me, Gideon picked up his menu and studied it. "What do you recommend?"

"The chicken-fried steak."

"No hesitation?"

"None." I smiled. "Luke makes the best gravy in the world."

"Luke?"

"He owns the place. He's also the cook."

"Who's Julia?" Gideon pointed to the words at the top of the menu.

"Luke's grandmother."

Alice returned to our table with two glasses of water. After setting them in front of us, she whipped out her order pad. "What'll you have?" She punctuated the question with a pop of her gum.

Gideon's gaze met with mine, and he said, "Two chicken-fried steak dinners, please."

"Anything to drink?"

"The lady will have—" he raised one eyebrow in question— "an orange Nehi."

I nodded.

"And I'll have a root beer, please."

Alice stuck her pencil behind her left ear. "I'll get those right out to you." With another pop of her gum, she was gone.

I leaned forward on my chair. "How did you know orange Nehi is my favorite?"

There was a subtle change in his expression, a look that made me feel warm clear down to my toes. When he spoke, his voice was low and intimate. "I pay attention to everything you do, Deb. Haven't you noticed?"

I knew then. Deep in my heart, I knew. I was falling in love with Gideon. I waited to feel the guilt, but it didn't come.

I didn't feel guilty.

I felt happy.

———

Mister Roberts was as wonderful as people had been saying. I loved hearing Gideon's laughter, deep and wonderfully male, and I loved hearing us laugh in unison. There was something very right about the sound. Something human and hopeful.

Throughout the movie, Gideon held my hand. Only when the credits were done rolling and the lights came up did he release it.

As we stood, I said, "I haven't laughed this much in a long while." I pressed my fingers to my cheeks. "My face actually hurts."

"Yeah, but a good kind of hurt."

I nodded.

Gideon took my arm as we started for the exit. "Want a piece of pie at Julia's?"

"No. I think I'd rather go on home."

"You should take it as a compliment."

"What?"

"That the folks around here care about you so much. They want to look out for you. They want to make certain I don't hurt you."

We stepped outside, pausing a moment beneath the colorful, dancing lights of the Rialto's marquee. The temperature had dropped while we were watching the film, and the air had a wintry bite to it. I pulled my sweater tighter about me.

"But, Deb . . . nobody cares about you more than I do." Gideon took hold of my shoulders with a gentle grasp. "It isn't possible that they could. I know that must sound crazy, but it's true." He drew me closer to him.

There, beneath those crazy pink, yellow, and green lights of the marquee, Gideon kissed me for all of Amethyst's watchful eyes to see . . .

And I didn't bother to ask God what He wanted me to do next.

Vera Beekman

My husband, Clyde, tells me I'm far too romantic for my own good. He may be right. Still, I thought it wonderful to see Deborah out on a date.

Now I hoped she would have wisdom and patience— two things often in short supply when a woman begins to care for a man.

CHAPTER EIGHT

November arrived.

I'd harvested and tilled my garden, preparing it for the coming of the first snowfall. I'd long since finished my canning for the season. All the jars of fruits and vegetables, properly labeled, were arranged on shelves in my cellar. I'd finished knitting the sweater that I'd started early in the summer, and I was in no hurry to begin a new project.

Suddenly there seemed too little to do to keep myself occupied. Too little except stare at the telephone each evening and command it to ring.

It didn't ring often enough.

Gideon didn't have a telephone of his own. He had to borrow his landlord's. To complicate matters, it was a toll call from Boise. Gideon was so close and yet he might as well have been living in Europe, as far away as he felt. It seemed even farther when the owner of that construction firm wanted Gideon to work more Saturdays. I was glad for Gideon. I knew he wanted to quit his sales job and do carpentry work full-time. Still, his extra work meant we couldn't see each other as frequently as we both wanted.

I found more and more excuses to drive into Boise during the week as well as on weekends. To shop. To have my hair done. To visit with my parents, often staying overnight, sometimes several nights in a row.

And always to see Gideon.

Always Gideon.

Oh, those hours together, all too brief as they seemed, were ambrosia for my hungry heart. We took long walks through the park on Sunday afternoons, holding hands, dried leaves crunching beneath our shoes, our breath forming misty clouds of white. We went to the drive-in theater on Friday nights but didn't see much of the movie; instead we kissed like a couple of teenagers, not stopping until we were both winded, almost dizzy. We talked about our childhoods, his brothers and nieces and nephews, my parents, our friends. We declared our hopes and dreams for the future. We laughed. We whispered sweet nothings.

It was marvelous.

It was anguish.

Isn't that always the way falling in love is?

Gideon braked his pickup to a halt in front of my parents' home. I could see the flicker of the television through a gap in the living room curtains. I suspected the gap was there because my mother had been watching for our return, the same as she'd done when I was seventeen.

"Look," Gideon said. "It's snowing."

I turned toward the front of the pickup and watched snow-flakes dancing in the headlights. It wasn't a sight I was glad to see. Snow meant difficult driving. Snow meant I might see Gideon even less frequently. Snow meant—

He put an arm around my shoulders and drew me close to his side, placing his lips near my ear. "I always wanted to live where it snowed in the winter."

"You're crazy," I said softly.

He nuzzled my neck. "Maybe."

I closed my eyes, enjoying the sensation.

"Deb . . ."

"Hmm?"

"I've got something to tell you."

"What?"

His voice dropped to a whisper. "I love you."

I stopped breathing.

He kissed my earlobe. "You must have known that's what I feel. I love you."

I hadn't realized how desperately I'd wanted to hear him say that until he did. All the sweet nothings he'd whispered before couldn't compare to those three little words.

"Deb, will you marry me?"

I opened my eyes to look at him, though he was only a shadow in the darkness of the truck's cab. My heart thundered in my chest.

"Marry me, Deb. Marry me soon. Make me the happiest guy in the world." He kissed my forehead, the tip of my nose, my mouth. "I've got a friend at work who has his own airplane. He told me he could fly us to Winnemucca, Nevada. There's no waiting to get married there. No blood tests. We could get a license, be married, and fly back all in the same day."

My thoughts were whirling. Was he truly saying these things or was I only imagining it? "Winnemucca?" The word was barely audible.

"Okay. Not Winnemucca then. But soon. We don't need a fancy wedding . . . unless that's what you want, of course. We can do whatever you want, Deb."

It was crazy, I suppose, to consider marrying again so soon. It was even crazier to consider marrying a man I'd known only a few months.

And yet . . . and yet my heart told me we were meant to be together. I wanted to follow my heart. I knew what love was, and I knew what marriage was. Why shouldn't we marry soon? There was no precise timetable for either.

If I married Gideon, there would be no more lonely nights, no more sleeping in a bed that was too large and too cold and too empty. If I married Gideon, I would have a partner to lean on when the world seemed to be crashing in upon me. I would have someone to cook dinner for and to talk to early on a Saturday morning before the sun came up. If I married Gideon . . .

"Say you will, Deb. I promise you'll never regret it. I'll be a good husband. I'll be a good provider. And if God wills, I'll be a good father. I love you."

A good husband . . .

A good provider . . .

A good father . . .

"If you're worried about the farm, you don't need to," Gideon continued, obviously trying to counter any argument before I could speak it. "We can close up the house for the winter.

Merle would see to the horses, and the land's already leased for next season. Right?"

"Yes."

"Well, then—"

"I said yes, Gideon."

He caught his breath, held it, then asked, "Yes, what? Yes, the land is leased? Or . . . " He let his words drift into silence.

"Yes, I will marry you, Gideon Clermont."

"You will?"

He sounded so disbelieving, I laughed softly before saying, "Yes, I will."

"Deb, I promise you won't ever be—"

I silenced his pledge with my index finger against his lips. "Shh. I know."

A heartbeat, two, and then he drew me close and kissed me, a kiss that was different from any we'd shared before.

Because suddenly *we* were different than we'd been before.

— *Bernice Richardson* —

What did I feel when Deborah and Gideon told her father and me they were engaged? A little stunned I suppose.

Although why I say that I haven't the foggiest notion. I've known from the first day I met Gideon Clermont how he felt about Deborah, and I'd have to be both blind and an idiot not to recognize her growing affection for him.

Certainly I saw more of my daughter in the weeks leading up to their engagement than I had in the past two years. And it wasn't because she had a sudden desire to spend more time with her mother!

Their romance did seem to develop rapidly, but I haven't

any objection to the two of them marrying. I have no reason to object. The more I've come to know Gideon, the more I like him. Besides, he's put a sparkle in Deborah's eyes again. That's worth just about anything.

After the surprise wore off, I confess I felt a tiny rush of excitement. There is something quite delightful about planning a wedding for one's daughter.

Deborah and Gideon said they weren't sure when they would wed. "Soon," was Deborah's answer when I pressed her for a date. "And small, Mother. Gideon and I agreed we want a small wedding. Just family and a few friends."

Well, I knew enough from the stubborn jut of my daughter's chin that I'd best leave it alone for the moment.

CHAPTER NINE

On Tuesday morning, I drove into town. At the corner of Second and Idaho, I parked my car in front of the Amethyst Community Church. I hadn't been to a worship service here in over a month since I'd spent every weekend in Boise.

But not only had I not been to services at Amethyst Community, I hadn't gone to church services anywhere else, either. After Saturday evenings out with Gideon, often not returning to my parents' house until two in the morning, it had been too easy to sleep late on Sundays. It hadn't seemed so unreasonable at the time, but now I felt uncomfortable.

"We can be Christians without going to church," I remembered Pastor Clyde preaching some time ago. *"But we make ourselves sick if we do. When we cut ourselves off from the body of Christ, we hurt both ourselves and the church. What good is a hand without an arm? What good is a foot without a leg? God has a place for each of us.*

That's why the Word tells us not to forsake meeting together. God wants us in fellowship. We gather because we need the whole body in order to accomplish the work set before us. We gather in order to encourage and instruct one another as we eagerly await the return of our Lord Jesus Christ."

I shook off the memory of that sermon. I didn't need to feel guilty about missing church for a few Sundays. I wasn't planning to make a habit of it. Soon I wouldn't be driving back and forth from the farm to Boise. Soon I would be living with Gideon as his wife. We would settle into a more normal life in Boise, and church attendance would be a regular part of that life.

I opened the car door to a blast of frigid November air. I shivered as I pulled the collar of my coat up to shield my neck, then got out and walked quickly toward the front door of the church.

Inside, I turned away from the sanctuary entrance and headed down the narrow hall toward the church office on the north side of the building. Before I reached it, I heard Pastor Clyde, talking in that gentle way that was uniquely his.

"Don't worry, Mrs. Humphrey. It's no inconvenience at all for me to drive out this afternoon . . . Yes . . . No . . . Of course . . . Well, then. I'll see you this afternoon . . . Good-bye."

The door to the office was open. I paused in the doorway and rapped lightly on the jamb.

Pastor Clyde looked up, smiled warmly, then stood. "Deborah! How good to see you."

"Are you busy?"

"Not too busy to see you, my dear. Come in." He motioned me forward. "Come in. It's been too long since we've had a chance to visit."

Again I felt a niggle of guilty discomfort, and again I pushed it away. In a town the size of Amethyst, I comforted myself, nothing much was secret. Pastor Clyde undoubtedly knew Merle Johnson had been tending my animals on the weekends, and he probably knew the reason why.

"Sit down, Deborah, and tell me how you're doing."

I took the indicated chair while Pastor Clyde regained his seat. He steepled his fingertips together in front of his chin, his elbows resting on the arms of the chair, and waited for me to begin.

"I . . . I have some news," I said at last.

He smiled, a silent encouragement.

"I'm engaged to be married."

I'd rarely seen Pastor Clyde reveal surprise—he was the calmest, most unflappable of men—but for the briefest moment, he showed it now. His eyebrows rose, his eyes widened, and his Adam's apple bobbed. Then the practice of many years of dealing with people came to his rescue, and he hid his surprise with such precision I wondered if I'd seen it after all.

"To Gideon Clermont," I added softly.

"I see." He leaned forward, placing his forearms on his desktop. "I look forward to meeting him, Deborah. You'll bring him to church with you soon, I hope."

"Yes, of course." I glanced down. Seeing a loose thread on my coat sleeve, I plucked at it. "I'll be moving to Boise after we're married. Gideon's work is there, and the commute is too far to do six days a week."

"I quite understand. Will you be selling the farm?"

I met his gaze again. "No." I shook my head slowly. "No, I won't sell. Owning the farm was Andy's dream, but I've come to love it just as much as he did. Gideon understands that. We'll be able to pay off the mortgage in a couple of years, maybe sooner if I find employment. Perhaps one day we can return to make our home here."

Pastor Clyde nodded, his expression thoughtful. After a lengthy silence, he said, "It sounds like you're planning to get married soon. Am I correct?"

"We haven't set a date . . . but, yes. We've agreed it will be a short engagement."

I felt the threat of tears, although I wasn't sure why. Perhaps because I was, once again, saying farewell to the life I'd known. I was going into a new life, one I wanted with my whole heart. But that didn't make the farewells any easier.

"I don't suppose it would do me any good to say it isn't wise to rush into marriage." Pastor Clyde's eyes narrowed ever so slightly. "Have you prayed about it, Deborah? Have you sought God's will?"

I clutched my hands together in my lap. "I believe God brought us together."

It was true. I did believe that. My heart told me Gideon was a gift in my life. He'd come to me when all I'd known was loss and heartache.

But had I prayed about marrying him? Had I sought God's will regarding when we should marry or where we should live?

No.

When had the silences between me and my Lord grown so long and so deep? I wondered.

Too long. Too deep.

I stood. "I'm afraid I can't stay, Pastor. But I . . . I wanted you to know before folks start talking about us." I gave an apologetic shrug. "You know how quickly news travels in Amethyst."

"Yes, I know." He stood, too. "Remember I'm only a phone call away if you need to talk."

"Thank you, Pastor. I appreciate it. I really do." With a half-hearted smile, I turned and left his office.

I had a raging headache by the time I arrived at the farm. I was upset that I'd said so few of the things I'd meant to say to Pastor Clyde, and I was frustrated because he hadn't rejoiced with me that I'd found love again. Instead, I'd been keenly aware of the undercurrent of things *he* hadn't said.

"So what was the point of my visit?" I muttered as I tossed my coat over the back of a kitchen chair.

Hoping a cup of tea would help ease the throbbing in my head, I filled the kettle with water from the faucet, then put it on the stove.

"I don't suppose it would do me any good to say it isn't wise to rush into marriage."

I pressed the heels of my hands against my temples and squeezed.

"Have you prayed about it, Deborah? Have you sought God's will?"

Would God have brought Gideon into my life if it weren't His will for us to be together? There were no impediments to marriage. We were both Christians. We would not be unequally yoked. We loved each other. We wanted to be together. We hadn't been unchaste. And anyway, wasn't it Paul who said it was better to marry than to burn?

I turned from the stove and stared out the window at the gray, wintry day. The trees along the border between my property and the Dailey farm stood like leafless sentinels. Dried remnants of last summer's crops lifted their heads above cold-hardened fields. The laying hens were inside the chicken coop, seeking warmth in their nests, and Daniel and Boone leaned their backsides against the barn, heads drooping.

A wave of loneliness swept over me, and I felt capsized by it. As if sensing my mood, Heidi appeared suddenly at my side, nudging my hand with her muzzle. I glanced down as I obligingly stroked her head.

"I'm ready to get on with my life," I whispered.

Heidi wagged her tail.

At least my dog seemed happy for me.

Pastor Clyde Beekman

There are a great many things I wanted to say to Deborah when she told me of her engagement. But I've learned a few things in my years in the ministry. I can recognize when my advice, no matter how much wisdom it might contain, is unwanted.

Deborah didn't want mine.

I have no reason to object to Gideon as her future husband. Though I haven't met the man, I've been told by others he is a likeable fellow, a hard worker, a Christian by all accounts, and devoted to Deborah. I also have no reason to doubt she loves him in return.

Still, I feel this nagging need to pray for her, especially for her protection in the storms of life that await her. It's a feeling I dare not ignore.

CHAPTER TEN

In the dream, I saw Andy as he was that last day of his life, smiling, his hair slightly disheveled, wearing overalls, a plaid flannel shirt, and sturdy work boots. We ate our lunch, and Andy told me a funny story, one Merle Johnson had told him earlier in the week. We talked about buying a television set, wondering if we could really afford the extravagance. We decided to buy a calf instead.

At last, lunch over, Andy got up from the table. "I'll get those last two tree stumps pulled this afternoon. It'll be good to have it over and done with."

He kissed my cheek, and I felt the bristle of his facial hair against my skin. Andy always had five o'clock shadow by noon. I teased him unmercifully about it.

As he walked out the kitchen door, the dream grew dark and foreboding. I tried to call out to him, tried to tell him to come back, to forget clearing that field. He didn't hear. He didn't stop. He didn't answer. I saw only his back as he walked away from me.

Andy . . .

Andy . . .

Andy . . .

The tractor was there, tipped onto its side. I ran toward it.

No!

No!

No!

But this time it wasn't Andy pinned beneath the machine. This time it wasn't Andy's lifeless eyes staring up at me.

"Gideon!" I cried as I bolted upright in bed, terror shooting through my veins.

Above the thunder of my heart, I heard Heidi's soft whimper and knew she had arisen from her rug to see what was wrong. But I could do nothing to reassure her. I couldn't even reassure myself. Not with the image of Gideon lying beneath the tractor still burned like a brand into my mind.

Was it a premonition of some sort?

A frisson of fear raced along my spine. I had survived losing Andy. Could I survive if I were to lose Gideon, too?

I clutched a pillow to my chest, then buried my face in it.

"Not Gideon. O God, not Gideon. Let me have Gideon. Please. Oh, please."

⌣

"Hello?" The voice on the other end of the line was definitely not a happy one.

"I need to speak to Gideon Clermont. Could you get him for me, please?"

"Lady, do you know what time it is?" He didn't wait for my answer. "It's barely seven."

"I'm sorry. I know it's early. I . . . I need to reach him before he leaves for work. I'm truly sorry, but it's important I talk to him. Please."

Maybe he heard the panic I still felt, several hours after the nightmare had awakened me, because his reply was slightly less grouchy. "Wait a minute. I'll get him for you."

I twisted the telephone cord, my stomach churning.

It seemed forever before Gideon answered. "Hello?"

"Gideon," I whispered.

"Deborah? What's wrong?"

"Nothing." *Everything!* I took a deep breath. "Gideon, is your friend still willing to fly us to Winnemucca to get married?"

"Is he—" A pause, then, "Yes."

"Then let's go. Let's get married."

"When?"

"Today," I answered. "Tomorrow. As soon as he can take us. I don't want to wait to plan a wedding. Not even a small one. Let's get married now."

Gideon chuckled softly. "Okay. Whatever you say. You know it's what I want. Pack a suitcase and then stay by the phone. I'll call you back as soon as I talk to Norm. He's the guy with the plane."

"Gideon?"

"Yeah?"

"I love you."

"I love you, too, Deb."

"Gideon?

"Yeah?"

"Drive careful."

"Sure thing. I'll call you as soon as I can."

Norman Adams

I'd have to say Deborah Haskin was the prettiest thing I ever saw come walking across a tarmac. Now I've always been partial to blondes with nice figures, both of which were sure true about her. But I think it was her bright smile and the sparkle of happiness in her blue eyes that made me think her so pretty.

My friend Gideon—I guess we'd known each other about eight or nine months by that time—had it bad for this gal, and seeing the two of them together . . . Well, I gotta say, it was almost enough to bring tears to my eyes, and I'm about the most unromantic man who ever drew breath. Just ask my wife. She'll confirm it for you.

I can't say the bride-to-be enjoyed our flight down to Winnemucca. It was obvious long before takeoff that Deborah was going to be a nervous flyer. I tried to ease her mind by telling her how safe air travel was these days. Hey, the first transcontinental round-trip flight took place this last May, made by an air force pilot in a North American F-86, New York City to Los Angeles and back again in one day. Funny thing is, I don't think she cared much about that aeronautic achievement. All she wanted was to get to Win-nemucca, preferably in one piece.

And me, my Cessna, and a bright, cloudless day came through for her and Gideon. Only a few bumps on takeoff and landing, but nothing serious.

Man, I love to fly.

CHAPTER ELEVEN

Gideon and I stood next to each other in the shadowy sanctuary, pale light filtering through a round stained-glass window above the altar. I'd been adamant that we must be married by a minister rather than a judge. I hadn't cared what denomination as long as the officiate was a Christian. It had taken five telephone calls for Gideon to find a minister who was available on such short notice.

But at last, there we were, holding hands, the minister standing before us, Norm Adams and the church secretary, our witnesses, standing behind us. The sanctuary was cold and drafty, and the minister's voice echoed in the high rafters of the otherwise silent church.

I remembered another wedding. It had been winter then, too—December—but the church had been bright with sunlight, poinsettias, and the joy of many family members and friends. My mother and father had tears in their eyes. My five bridesmaids had looked resplendent in gowns of Christmas green. And I had looked every bit the bride in my gown of satin, lace, and pearls.

Today I wore a gold sweater and a brown wool skirt. Not the least bit bridal in appearance.

Gideon squeezed my icy fingers. I looked up, and he smiled. Suddenly I felt warmed. It didn't matter what I wore or who was with us. All that mattered was that we were about to become man and wife.

God brought you to me, Gideon, and then you brought happiness into a tearful heart. I love you. I don't think I'll ever stop loving Andy, but it won't lessen the love I feel for you from this day forward.

In our turns, we repeated our vows, promising our love and fidelity until death. I didn't allow myself to remember the part death had played in my first marriage.

This was a day for hope.

With the sounds of slot machines whirring and clanging in the background, Norm toasted us with champagne in the restaurant of the hotel where we were staying. We ordered food, but I don't think any of us ate much. At least I didn't. I was nervous about the wedding night to come. One would have thought I was eighteen and innocent rather than thirty-one and widowed.

I was both glad and sorry when Norm made his excuses and left the restaurant.

"He's a good Joe." Gideon poured more champagne into his glass. "He wouldn't let me pay him for the flight down here or for his room for the night. Said it's his wedding gift to us. That and this bottle of champagne. Sure you don't want any? Not even one sip?"

I shook my head.

"This bothers you, doesn't it?" He lifted the glass slightly as he spoke.

Would it sound petty to admit it *did* bother me?

I recalled Andy telling my father he'd seen too much drinking while in the army. He'd said he never knew liquor to improve either a person or a situation.

Ashamed that my thoughts had strayed once again to my deceased husband instead of remaining on my groom, I dropped my gaze to the plate before me.

"Deb, if it bothers you for me to have a glass of champagne, I won't drink it."

I looked up again to see him shoving both glass and bottle to the far side of the table.

He leaned toward me. "I want to make you happy, Deborah Clermont. Now and always."

PART TWO

1956

But where then is my hope?

Can anyone find it?

JOB 17:15

CHAPTER TWELVE

April

The heels of my shoes clicked smartly against the concrete as
I walked toward our apartment in the north end of Boise. Tree
limbs, adorned in the lime green leaves of early spring, formed a
canopy over my head, causing sunlight to cavort with shadows
on the sidewalk before me.

In nice weather like today, it was only a ten-minute walk
from the downtown office building where I worked to our
apartment, a converted detached garage behind an elegant three-
story home on Harrison Boulevard. Our place was . . . cozy.
It had barely enough room for two people and a dog. Actually,
there wasn't room for a dog the size of Heidi, but somehow
we managed.

When I turned the corner, I was surprised to see Gideon's
pickup parked at the curb. I usually had time to start dinner
before he arrived home from work.

"Gideon," I called as I opened the door. "What are you—"

"Happy anniversary!"

I barely heard his voice before he swept me off my feet and twirled me around. Heidi barked, wanting to be part of the gaiety.

"Five months already," Gideon whispered. "Can you believe it?" Then he kissed me. Thoroughly, completely kissed me.

I was winded by the time our lips parted.

"I've got great news, Deb."

I tightened my arms around his waist to keep him close. "What?"

"My boss is giving the whole crew a bonus. We finished the job ahead of schedule and under budget. He said he wanted to reward us for the good work." He kissed the tip of my nose. "We'll be able to pay off the mortgage on the farm now instead of next fall."

I drew back slightly so I could look into his eyes. "Are you joking?"

"No." His grin broadened. "I'm not joking. A week or two from now, we'll be debt free."

"I need to pinch myself." Truly, my legs felt rubbery. I moved to sit on the sofa, holding Gideon's hand and drawing him with me.

The bonus was one more in a string of good things that had happened since the day we got married. We'd sold the laying hens and my car within two days of our return from Winnemucca, and Merle Johnson had been more than obliging about caring for Daniel and Boone as long as we needed him to. We'd rented this little apartment before the first week of marriage was out, and I'd found employment with a small accounting firm in Boise the week after that. Four days later, on the day after

Thanksgiving, Gideon had been offered full-time work with the construction company he'd been working for on Saturdays—at twice what he'd been earning as a salesman!

We weren't rich by any stretch of the imagination, but with both of us working, we'd been able to pay off our debts. The mortgage on the farm was the last of them.

Gideon squeezed my shoulders. "We should go out to celebrate."

Before I could answer, Heidi plopped her head onto my thigh and looked up at me with soulful eyes, her tail wagging.

Gideon scratched her behind an ear. "I think it's time we thought about getting a bigger place. One with a large fenced yard for Heidi. Our lease will be up in June. If we start looking right away, maybe we could move by then."

"It would be nice to turn around without bumping into something." I sighed. "But we've been so happy here."

"True enough."

I closed my eyes and rested my head against his chest, feeling content.

After a lengthy silence, Gideon said, "I stopped and looked at some houses up in the foothills before I came home."

"Up in the Highlands subdivision?" I couldn't help laughing. "Oh, you *are* dreaming big, Mr. Clermont. There aren't any places we could afford to rent up there."

"I was thinking more along the lines of buying a home up there, not renting one."

I straightened. "Buy a place in the Highlands? Gideon, we couldn't possibly. They're too expensive. The bank wouldn't even consider loaning to us. Neither one of us has been at our job for a year, and even if that didn't matter, we'd need a sizeable down payment, which we don't have."

"We'd have the money if we sold the farm."

I was struck dumb.

"Don't look at me like that, Deb. Think about it. Our jobs are here in Boise. We're happy living in town. What's the likelihood we'll choose to live in the country again? Ever. What good is the farm to us except as an investment?"

"I don't know if we will ever want to live there." I pushed up from the couch and walked into the kitchenette, an extension of the tiny living room. "But I don't want to sell the farm. It was—" I stopped the words in my throat before they could escape.

Gideon understood anyway. "It was Andy's dream to own a farm. I know. So you've told me." He stared at me hard. "But Andy's gone. It's *our* dreams we need to think about now. Yours and mine together."

"I'm not ready to sell it, Gideon. I can't explain it. I'm just not ready."

"Deb, be reasonable."

"I'm being perfectly reasonable." I didn't sound like it. My voice was strident, the volume on the rise. "And I'm *not* going to sell the farm."

He held out a hand toward me. "Let me take you up to the Highlands and drive through the subdivision. There's a couple of houses I know we could afford. They look like palaces compared to this place. If you could see them—"

"We can't afford a home up there without a large down payment." There was no mistaking my anger. "You said so yourself. And we don't have a large down payment to make."

"Can't we even *talk* about it?" He sounded angry, too.

"No."

Gideon raked the fingers of his right hand through his hair.

"What's wrong with you, Deb? I've never known you to be stubborn before."

"I can be very stubborn, Gideon Clermont. My parents could have told you that." Tears flooded my eyes, which only made me more angry. I didn't want to cry. I didn't feel sad. I wanted to be heard, and I wanted to be understood. "And no matter what you have to say, I will *not* sell the farm."

Gideon released a strangled sound of frustration, then muttered, "Women!" before storming out of the house, slamming the door behind him.

The silence was deafening.

I didn't know whether to let my tears fall or throw something in rage.

Clarice Andrus

My husband and I have lived in our home on Harrison Boulevard for the past ten years. It was the previous owners who converted the detached garage into a rental unit. I never would have done so. Renting can be such a trying business. So difficult to find reputable people. And when such people are living in one's own backyard . . .

Well, you can understand my feelings, I'm sure.

The Clermonts were an exception to the rule. I knew it the moment I laid eyes on them, and they proved my instincts true in the months they rented the cottage. (*Cottage* sounds so much better than *apartment* or *converted garage*. Don't you think?)

Deborah Clermont has a flare for decorating on a budget. She made new curtains for all of the windows. Nothing fancy, mind you. *Cheery* would be a good description of the home she made for them.

Cheery would also be a good description for Deborah herself. So pleasant and obviously happy. Her joy as a new bride was contagious. Being around her made even *me* feel about twenty years old again.

And Gideon Clermont? Well, he was a godsend. Ever since my husband's heart attack three years ago, it was more and more difficult for him to do the little odd jobs that all homes require. Gideon stepped in to fill that gap on more than one occasion. He wouldn't let us pay him one red cent for the work he did either.

They seemed well matched, those two. Which was why I was so surprised that night I saw Gideon storm out of the cottage, slamming the door behind him. There was no mistaking his anger. I swear, there could have been smoke coming out of his ears. He strode to the curb, got into his truck, gunned the engine, and roared away.

Most unlike him.

I was still standing on the back patio, staring at the street, when the cottage door opened a second time and Deborah appeared in the doorway. I'm not certain, since my eyesight isn't what it used to be, but I believe she was crying. When our gazes met across the yard, she gave me a halfhearted smile, then ducked back inside.

It was after midnight before I heard Gideon's truck return.

CHAPTER THIRTEEN

I pretended to be asleep when Gideon entered our bedroom at 12:57 A.M.

I heard him run into something as he rounded the end of the bed. If his muffled groan was any indication, he'd stubbed his toe or banged his shin.

Good. It serves you right. I hope it hurts all night long.

Clutching a pillow to my chest, I rolled onto my right side, my back toward the center of the bed. I heard Gideon drop his clothes onto the nearby straight-backed chair. A familiar sound, yes, but never one I'd listened to under these circumstances. Since the day of our wedding, we'd retired each night together, sometimes lying awake and talking into the wee hours.

This silence between us was something new.

Gideon slid between the sheets, clad now in his pajamas. He lay very still for a while, and I held my breath, waiting. Then he rolled onto his left side, his back toward me. I didn't have to see to know that was what he'd done. I simply knew it.

How could he be so stubborn and obstinate? How could he ask me to sell the farm when he knew what it meant to me?

He has *helped to pay off the mortgage earlier than expected.*

True enough. But I would have been able to do it on my own, given a little more time. I could have done it without impacting our finances. I was working, too. My salary contributed to our livelihood.

But no matter how angry I was, I hadn't been the one to leave and stay out for hours without so much as a by-your-leave. Where had he been all this time? Why hadn't he called me? He must have known I'd be worried. How could he treat me so shabbily?

I caught my breath again and listened.

Gideon was snoring! He'd fallen asleep while I lay there in misery, and he was snoring.

I wanted nothing so much as to smack him—*hard!*—with my pillow.

I slept some, but my mood had not improved by the time the alarm clock jangled stridently in my ear. I silenced it with a quick gesture. Gideon didn't budge.

The louse!

I shoved aside the blankets and hurried into the bathroom. It was the smallest of spaces, barely room for the narrow shower stall, toilet, and sink. I glanced at my reflection in the medicine-cabinet mirror, groaned at the woman who stared back at me, then shucked off my nightclothes, put on a shower cap, and turned on the water and got into the shower.

I stood beneath the hot spray and listened to the clang and groan of the pipes. I could admit it would be nice to live in a newer home, one with a bathtub and a living room that was separate from the kitchen, and a bedroom where no one smashed toes or banged shins in the dark.

Yes, it would be nice. But I still couldn't and wouldn't sell the farm. It was partly to do with Andy, of course, with the love he and I had shared for those forty acres, with keeping his dreams alive even though he was gone. But it was more than that, too.

I closed my eyes, envisioning the farm as it came to life in the spring. I loved the smells and sounds of the farm. I loved seeing Daniel and Boone looking sleek after losing their winter coats. I loved the drive into Amethyst when colts or calves or lambs frolicked in nearly every pasture. I loved the sound of lowing cows coming from the Johnson place at milking time. I loved absolutely everything about it.

Then I remembered the way Gideon had held and comforted me when I was feeling blue last month on the anniversary of Andy's death. Gideon had said he understood that. He'd said he knew my love for him wasn't lessened because of the love I'd had for Andy. I'd thought him both wise and wonderful and incredibly mature.

So why was he being so unreasonable, so immature, now?

I lathered myself with the bar of soap, rinsed, then turned off the water before I drained the hot-water tank. It wouldn't improve the situation between me and my husband if he was forced to take a cold shower because I lingered too long.

By the time I exited the bathroom, wrapped in a terry-cloth bathrobe, Gideon was sitting on the side of the bed. He gripped his head between his hands, his elbows resting on his thighs.

"I'm through," I said.

He straightened, then looked at me over his shoulder. "Thanks," he muttered.

"Headache?"

He grunted as he rose from the bed.

Serves you right, Gideon Clermont.

I left the bedroom, feeling worse by the minute. Even in my anger, I realized I was being self-righteous and contentious.

But at least I have good cause.

With practiced efficiency, I started the coffee brewing, then prepared sandwiches for our lunch boxes. Next I dropped two slices of bread into the toaster. By the time they popped up and were buttered, the coffee was ready. I grabbed two mugs from the cupboard, and as if on cue, Gideon appeared through the bedroom doorway.

Normally, I handed him his coffee mug and received a kiss during the exchange. This morning, I left the mug on the counter and moved out of his way, keeping my eyes averted as I headed for the bedroom to dress for work.

Why didn't he say something? Why didn't he come after me? Why didn't he apologize?

I was miserable.

I shed my bathrobe, donned my underclothes, hose, and satin slip, then grabbed a yellow shirtwaist dress from the minuscule closet.

If we bought a house in the Highlands, my closet wouldn't have to be minuscule.

I frowned. There would be no owning a house yet, not unless we sold the farm—which we weren't going to do. Which *I* wasn't going to do. The farm was mine, and keeping it or selling it was my decision to make. Perhaps if Gideon hadn't stormed out of here last night, we could have come to an understanding. If he had returned and talked to me . . .

Where was he until nearly one?

A shiver of dread went through me. Multiple reasons lurked just beyond my willingness to entertain them.

How could you do this to me, Gideon?

Fighting tears and a lump in my throat, I put on my shoes, grabbed my purse, and returned to the kitchenette. My toast and coffee went untouched. I had no stomach for either of them.

"I'm going to leave now," I said softly.

"Why don't you wait? I'll drive you."

I glanced at him but gave my head a quick shake.

He frowned. "Let's not argue anymore."

I didn't want to argue either, but I wasn't ready to forgive him. Not just yet.

"Deb, I don't want to fight. I'm sorry." He rubbed his temples with his fingertips. "I was wrong. I shouldn't have left like that."

I swallowed hard, then asked, "Where did you go?"

"Some of the guys from the job . . . I knew where they'd be. They'd gone out to celebrate the bonus. I joined them."

I waited in silence.

"We were at a bar and grill over on State Street."

"You spent the whole evening in a bar?"

"We had a few brews and shot pool. It gave me some time to get over being mad."

I looked at him a little more closely. His eyes were blood-shot. I wanted to ask him how many *brews* he'd had, but then again, I didn't want to fight anymore.

He must have read my thoughts for he came to me then, wrapped me in his arms, and said, "Please forgive me. I'm sorry.

I was wrong to leave, and I was wrong not to call you after I did. I won't ever walk out on you like that again. I love you."

"And I love you." I pressed my face against his chest. "Forgive me, too?"

"You know it." He kissed the top of my head and held me closer. "We'll go out to dinner tonight to celebrate. Okay?"

"Okay."

We stayed like that for a short while, clinging to each other, but finally we had to break apart, get our things, and head out the door to our respective jobs.

We rode toward downtown in silence. I suppose neither of us knew what to say next. Perhaps both of us felt the peace between us was too fragile.

As we passed the gray stone church on the corner three blocks from where I worked, I had a sudden longing to go inside, sit down in one of the pews, and talk to God. How long had it been since I'd been inside of a church? Weeks. No, it had been months.

"We can be Christians without going to church." I could almost see Pastor Clyde as his words, spoken long ago, repeated in my head. *"But we make ourselves sick if we do."*

I flinched with guilt.

We haven't had time to find a church, I silently argued.

It's a wonder I didn't laugh aloud at the ludicrousness of that argument. How did one go about finding a church when one wasn't looking?

But we *had* been busy since we got married, closing up the house at the farm, moving into our little apartment, settling into new jobs. Surely God understood how overwhelming it was, how little time was left for Gideon and me to be together.

We'll do better. Next Sunday, we'll go to church.

— Norman Adams —

Okay, so most of the crew tied one on after we found out about the bonuses. Most of us paid for it, too. We dragged onto the job the next morning, suffering from our hangovers and too little sleep but still mighty happy about the extra money coming in our next paychecks.

I was real glad the night before when Gideon joined us at Shenanigans Bar and Grill. Didn't expect him to. He'd been tied to Deborah's pretty little apron strings ever since he got hitched. He talked about her all the time. Couldn't seem to get enough of her. Crazy in love.

But one look at his face when he came into the bar, and I put two and two together: A fight with the little woman. It was clear Gideon was nursing a grudge—right along with his beer—but he didn't want to talk about it. At least not then.

The next day he let something slip that told me more than he probably meant for me to know. I asked him if he'd patched things up with Deborah. He told me he had. Then he said, "Norm, tell me something. How does a man compete with a dead guy, especially one who was perfect?"

I asked him what he meant—even though I knew he must be talking about Deborah's first husband—but he clammed up after that. Just started swinging his hammer with a vengeance.

I guess he didn't patch things up after all. Not inside himself, anyway.

CHAPTER FOURTEEN

Gideon and I visited the small gray stone church, Grace Chapel, on the Sunday after our fight. The sermon that morning was on sacrificial giving. I'd thought it scripturally sound, though not exciting.

When we left, Gideon said, "He was sure scolding somebody real good. They'd better start paying their tithes."

We didn't go back.

Gideon didn't care for the service at the church on the northwest corner of Tenth and State, which we visited on the following Sunday, either; the minister was "in his dotage." The week after that, the members of the church on the northeast corner of the same intersection proved "too uppity for their own good," and the service at the church one block east of there, where we visited next, was "too ritualistic."

We slept in on the Sunday morning after that . . . and the one after that . . . and the one after that.

With the coming of spring and more daylight hours, Gideon worked longer days, six days a week. Sunday was the one day that was exclusively ours. We were newlyweds, still growing accustomed to each other. Was it so terrible we wanted to spend that day together? And didn't the Bible tell me I should submit to the wishes of my husband? We would find a church eventually. It didn't have to be right away.

The guilt I'd felt so keenly in April was forgotten by June.

— Jack Clermont —

While my business trip to Washington State wasn't my doing, the drive back to California via Boise was. The entire Clermont clan expected a report on the woman my baby brother married almost seven months earlier.

Of course, Mom has talked to Deborah quite a bit over the telephone, and they've exchanged quite a few letters. (Deborah's a much better correspondent than Gideon, that's for certain.) But what we all wanted was some firsthand knowledge about her. That was my assignment. Get the inside scoop on Deborah Clermont.

The directions Gideon gave me were easy enough to follow, and I arrived at their place a little after two o'clock on Saturday afternoon. Gideon was at the curb before I could shut off my Buick's engine, and the instant I was out of the car, he was hugging me and slapping me on the back. We've always been a family that shows affection easily, Gideon even more than the rest of us.

It was sure good to see him.

My brother's put on a bit of weight in the year and a half since I last saw him. But it's the good kind of weight gain.

He's well muscled and healthy-looking. Judging by the strip of white skin along his hairline, he's been to the barbershop recently. The latter was no doubt due to the pretty woman who appeared moments later to shake my hand and welcome me to their home.

A good influence *and* a good cook. Looks like Gideon hit the jackpot.

CHAPTER FIFTEEN

It wasn't Jack's fault—he was as warm and charming as his younger brother—but for the first hour or so, I felt like a bug being
inspected under a microscope. Eventually the conversation turned
to the youthful exploits of the three Clermont boys, and I was
able to relax and enjoy the visit. More than enjoy. As the childhood stories unfolded, I laughed so much my sides hurt and my
cheeks ached.

They told about the time Gideon and Jack got into a shoving
match in the kitchen. Losing his temper completely, Jack went
to punch Gideon in the stomach, but Gideon grabbed a cast iron
skillet off the stove in the nick of time, putting it over his belly.
Jack thought he'd broken his hand, he hit the frying pan so hard.
Before Jack quit screaming in pain, Gideon was out the back
door and long gone.

They told about the time the three brothers—ages twelve,
eleven, and eight—snuck into the movie theater through the

back alley and then, in a panic when they heard someone coming, closed themselves in a storage closet. They got locked in. After they were found and their parents' panic had subsided, their mother made them spend four consecutive Saturdays cleaning the theater's lobby area from top to bottom.

They told about the time Jack and Bob, the middle brother, convinced Gideon, the baby, that he could fly off the garage roof with a pair of plywood wings Jack had made in shop class. He was the littlest, they said, and the updraft would carry him better than the older and bigger boys. Of course, no updraft caught him. Gideon and the wings crashed to earth like a rock. Gideon figured he got off easy with only a broken left arm. His brothers received more serious punishment from their dad.

Those were only a few of the stories I heard. I found myself half the time being grateful I was an only child and the other half wishing I had siblings. They made it sound horrible and wonderful at the same time.

Famished after several hours of nonstop talk, the three of us went out for dinner at a downtown café known for its delicious pies. Our entrees were good, too, but it was the hot cherry pie á la mode and the rich dark coffee we lingered over, the men still reminiscing and me still listening.

I was feeling rather mellow and a bit overstuffed when Gideon excused himself from the table and headed for the restrooms at the back of the café.

"Deb," Jack said, "I've got to thank you. You've made my brother one happy guy. It's like he's a whole new person."

I smiled at the compliment.

"I was kind of worried about him after he got out of the army."

"Worried? Why?"

"Oh, little things. He seemed to be without a rudder. Restless. No direction. He couldn't find work and had a lot of time on his hands. He didn't have a steady girl, either, and most of his buddies were still in the army. He was drinking too much and staying out too late at night."

"Drinking too much?" I echoed softly, feeling a shiver move up my spine as I remembered the night Gideon and I had argued about the farm. He'd definitely had too much to drink that night, and he'd had a whale of a hangover the next morning. What if—

"Yeah," Jack responded, interrupting my thoughts. "But it was boredom more than anything, I guess. Whatever was bothering him then, he's over it now. He's a different guy today than the fellow who left California. I've never seen him looking this good or this happy. And he loves you. That's as clear as the nose on your face."

The tension left my shoulders. How silly I was to react—to *over*react—the way I had to Jack's remark about Gideon's drinking. I really had to curb this habit of letting my imagination run wild over the smallest things.

Jack stayed the night on the sofa in our living room. He was too tall and the couch was too short, but he insisted he would be fine. Nonetheless, I felt guilty. If we had a bigger house, we would also have a guest room.

Later, as I lay in the circle of Gideon's arms, my head on his shoulder, pale moonlight falling through the open window to pool on the foot of our bed, I whispered, "I like Jack a lot."

"He's okay for an older brother." There was a smile in his voice.

I turned my head so I could see his face in the silvery light. "I've decided your mother is a saint if she had to put up with you three for thirty-some-odd years, and I mean to tell her so when I write her next."

"What do you think about you and me taking a trip down to California this summer?" Gideon kissed my forehead. "Then you could meet the whole family. They'll all love you, same as Jack does. Hey, maybe we could go visit that new Disneyland park everybody's been talking about. Do you think you could get some time off work?"

"I think so. It would be without pay since I haven't been there all that long, but I'm sure they'd let me have the time off. Summer's a slower time of year for accounting firms anyway."

"Good. We'll tell Jack in the morning."

I yawned, then said a tired, "Okay."

Contented, I was sound asleep within moments.

— *Bernice Richardson* —

I wasn't happy when Deborah and Gideon ran off to Nevada for one of those quickie weddings. It didn't seem like the right and proper way for a marriage to begin. Besides, it spoiled all my plans for a beautiful church wedding.

I'll confess, I was a bit concerned about *why* they chose to elope. I was eager for grandchildren, but I didn't want any babies arriving before Deborah had been married at least nine months.

However, after seven months had passed since the two of them got married, I was more than a little impatient for news that Deborah was expecting a baby. All of the women in my church circle have grandbabies to love and to spoil. I wanted the same. I'm not getting any younger, you know.

When Deborah told me Gideon wanted to sell her farm so they could buy a house in town, I thought it sounded reasonable. Then she told me she refused . . .

Well, I simply could *not* believe it.

"Deborah," I told her, "you need a home. You won't want to work forever. It's time for you to have children, and you'll need more rooms than you have now."

"Mother," she replied, rolling her eyes as she did so, "I promise not to raise your grandchildren in a converted garage. Okay? When the time comes, Gideon and I will have a home of our own."

With that, she put an effective end to the discussion.

I was frustrated beyond words.

CHAPTER SIXTEEN

I didn't mean to tell Mother about Gideon's desire to sell the farm and buy a house in the Highlands. I'm not sure how it happened. We were shopping together on a Saturday morning and stopped to have lunch in the restaurant of The Bon Marche. We talked about any number of things, and the next thing I knew, I had told her about Gideon's bonus, paying off the farm mortgage, our argument and how we'd made up.

Fortunately, Mother didn't berate me for being foolish, although that was clearly what she thought of my stance. Instead, the conversation made an abrupt shift to the grandchild she wanted.

That was a dangerous moment for me, and my escape was nothing short of miraculous. But I couldn't very well tell my mother I thought I was pregnant before I had a chance to tell Gideon—which I planned to do that night.

A pot roast, simmering with onions, carrots, and potatoes, was in the oven. The table was covered with a pale blue tablecloth and set with fine china, crystal, and silverware. Candles flickered throughout the living room and kitchen, and soft music played from the phonograph.

Gideon was late. Later than usual.

Several times I walked to the window and looked toward the curb, as if I could make his truck instantly appear by wishing it there.

Could something be wrong?

I checked my wristwatch, then returned to the stove.

Should I turn off the oven? The pot roast was cooked through, the vegetables tender and juicy. If I waited—

I heard the familiar rumble of the truck's engine and breathed a sigh of relief. Gideon was home.

With hurried steps, I went into the bathroom and checked my appearance in the medicine-cabinet mirror. I tied a chiffon scarf around the base of my ponytail and freshened my lipstick. I suddenly wished I'd put on a dress, but it was too late now. Heart pounding, I returned to the living room.

O God, please let him be as excited about the baby as I am.

When we were first married, Gideon and I had talked often about the family we hoped to have. Should we have two children, four children, more? But as the months passed, those conversations had dwindled. Perhaps we'd both been afraid I couldn't conceive. After all, I'd been married to Andy for fifteen months without a pregnancy. But now—

The door opened, and Gideon took one step inside. He stopped, looked around the room, blinked, then said, "Well, look at this. Did I forget an anniversary or something?"

"No." I smiled as I moved toward him for a welcome-home kiss.

At the last possible moment, Gideon turned his head slightly so that my lips grazed his cheek. "Sorry. I think I may be getting a cold. Don't want you to catch it from me if I am."

I had the strangest feeling something wasn't right. As if the world had suddenly shifted on its axis. What was it that troubled me?

"Hmm." Gideon gave my shoulder a light squeeze, then walked toward the stove. "Something sure smells good." He opened the oven door. "Pot roast?"

"Yes."

"You sure I didn't miss an anniversary? It isn't your birthday, is it?" Still bending over the oven, he looked at me with a puppy-dog-I-just-want-to-please-you-and-you-know-you-can't-resist-me expression.

The world shifted back into its proper place.

"No," I said, smiling at him. He knew me well. I couldn't resist him. "You didn't miss an anniversary and it isn't my birthday. I wanted to . . . surprise you with a nice dinner." *And a little bit of news.* "That's all."

He closed the oven door. "Well, I *am* surprised, Deb, and I'm also starving. Give me a minute to wash up. Be right back."

Gideon was talkative over dinner. More so than usual. He told me all about the new office building they were working on. He told me about one of his coworkers who was getting married later in the summer. He told me about Norm Adams's latest flight, this time to Alaska.

Finally, after we'd eaten our fill and the candles had burned low, it was my turn.

"I went downtown with Mother today."

"Uh-oh. What'd you buy?"

"Nothing. We were window-shopping."

"Whew. I thought I was being buttered up for some major purchase."

I gave him a stern glance. "When have I ever done such a thing?"

"Never. But I hear the guys talking at work. The tricks some of their wives pull would curl your hair."

"Oh, really." We had veered offtrack with this conversation, and somehow I needed to get us going in the right direction again. "Mother was wondering how long we plan to live here."

"Did you tell her forever? The place does sort of grow on a fellow."

"Well . . . " The butterflies returned to my stomach. "I may have been wrong. We ought to think about moving before next winter."

Gideon leaned forward and blew out a sputtering candle before asking, "Why's that?"

"Because—" I took a quick breath— "we're going to need another bedroom."

Gideon met my gaze again.

"For the baby," I added softly.

"The baby?"

I nodded as I pressed my hands against my abdomen.

"You're going to have a baby?"

"*We* are."

"When?"

"January, I think. I won't be sure until I've seen the doctor."

"A baby." He spoke the word with wonder. "I'm going to be a dad?"

I waited what seemed a long while before I said, "Yes. Are you happy about it, Gideon?"

"Ah, Deb. Don't you know the answer to that already?" He rose and came to me, pulling me up from my chair with a gentle grasp on my arms. "I couldn't be happier. You're having my baby." He kissed me, long, slow, sweet. "It's the best news in the world," he whispered near my ear once the kiss ended. "The absolute best."

Perhaps that was the moment I should have agreed to sell the farm. But I didn't.

Janelle Burns

Deborah and I met at the accounting firm where we both worked. I was there about six months before she was hired. I was the receptionist. Deborah was one of the three secretaries.

A couple of weeks before Christmas—she'd worked there about three weeks by that time—I asked where she and her husband went to church, and she told me they hadn't found one to attend yet. I invited the Clermonts to go with me and my husband to our church's Christmas program, but they weren't able to attend.

In the months that followed, Deborah and I often ate our sandwiches together in the break room on the second floor of our office. We talked about many things during those lunch hours, but my favorite topic of conversation was always the Lord.

Deborah? I ascertained rather early in our friendship that

she'd made a commitment to Christ, but I also discerned she wasn't walking with Him at the time. That's an unhappy condition to be in for a believer—knowing Jesus but doing our best to ignore Him. I've seen it happen to others.

I didn't know what else to do but try to live out my faith with integrity before her. I offered her my friendship with an open hand. I prayed she would see Jesus in me, and in seeing Him, her heart's cry would be for restoration with her Master.

Deborah was a newlywed, and her head was in the clouds over her husband. I may have been married fifteen years, but I remember well enough what those first months of marriage were like. My husband, Ted, still makes my heart go pitter-pat when he walks into a room. Yet, it's our steadfast devotion to God that has made our marriage remain strong through the trials of life.

And there have been trials. There will always be trials. It's part of the refining process.

CHAPTER SEVENTEEN

I enjoyed my job at Cooper, Smith, and Peevey, CPAs. The people were pleasant and friendly, and for the most part, my work was interesting. Still, when I walked through the office doorway on Monday morning, I was mentally counting down the months until I could stay home with the baby.

Joy welled up within me, the same feeling that had over-whelmed me time and again this weekend. And Gideon's gladness over my pregnancy increased my own tenfold.

When he drove me to work that morning, Gideon had insisted I call for an appointment as soon as the doctor's office opened. I suspected my husband would be spoiling me over the course of my pregnancy. Not a bad thing to have happen. I loved to be spoiled.

Janelle, the office receptionist, looked up from her desk. "Good morning, Deborah."

"Good morning."

"How was your weekend?"

"Grand." I beamed. "Absolutely grand."

Her eyes narrowed slightly, and she cocked her head to one side. "What's up?"

"Nothing," I lied, even as my smile broadened.

The phone rang before Janelle could call me on the falsehood. A temporary reprieve. She would worm it out of me by the lunch hour.

Not that I intended to keep my pregnancy a secret. Now that Gideon knew, I wanted to tell the world. In fact, we were going over to my parents' home that night so we could tell them the news in person.

I walked down the wide, well-lit hallway to my office, across the hall from my boss. The room was small, but it had a north-facing window with a nice view of the mountain range. I dropped my purse into the bottom drawer of my desk, then checked my desk calendar for any appointments. None, thank goodness. Perhaps I'd be able to catch up on some filing.

"Well?" Janelle whispered from my doorway. "What is it? What aren't you telling me?"

I shook my head, suppressing laughter. "You'll have to wait until lunch."

"You're a cruel woman, Deborah."

I was saved a second time by the ringing telephone. Janelle hurried away to answer it.

I rose and closed my office door.

I tried hard to stay focused on my work over the next hour and a half, but it wasn't easy to do. Not when I kept checking the wall clock, waiting for the doctor's office to open so I could make my appointment.

At twenty after nine, a soft rap sounded on my door.

"Yes?"

The door opened, but instead of a person, what I saw was a beautiful bouquet of long-stemmed red roses, a dozen in all, plus one blue and one pink carnation. The bouquet moved toward me, carried by Janelle.

As soon as she set the vase on my desk, she said, "I will *not* wait until lunch."

Heart thumping, I reached for the tiny envelope, opened it, and pulled out the card.

To the mother of my child. I love you now. I'll love you always. Gideon

I could barely read the words for the tears that filled my eyes.

"Deborah? What is it?"

"I'm okay." I sniffed and reached blindly for a tissue. "It's something good." I wiped the tears from beneath my eyes with a handkerchief, then blew my nose. "The flowers are from Gideon."

"I figured that much."

I smiled even as more tears formed. "We're going to have a baby."

Janelle let out a squeal that brought the other two secretaries and one of the accountants to my office doorway. By then, Janelle was hugging me.

"What is it?"

"What's wrong?"

"Look at those roses!"

"It's a secret," Janelle said as she released me.

But, of course, even if it was meant to be a secret, there was no keeping it one now.

I fairly floated on a cloud of happiness into my parents' home that evening. If I hadn't been holding on to Gideon's arm, I might have drifted away, like a helium-filled balloon escaping a child's grasp.

What Mother hadn't guessed on Saturday, she didn't miss now. She heard the first few words out of my mouth, saw the bliss on our faces, and instantly came up with *Baby!*

"Oh, darling!" She jumped up from the davenport. "I'm so happy for you both!" She hugged me, then Gideon, then me again, and finally Dad.

If I hadn't already been overjoyed about my pregnancy, seeing Mother's reaction would have made me so. Her eyes sparkled, and she didn't stop smiling the whole time we were there. She wanted to know when the baby was due and what names were we considering if it was a boy and what names if a girl and who was my doctor and how long did I intend to keep working. I had few answers for her, but it didn't seem to matter.

Dad and Gideon stood off to one side of the room, neither of them saying much. Dad liked to stay out of the way when the women in his life were giddy with joy.

Henry Richardson

The night Deborah and Gideon told us about the baby, I knew Gideon had been drinking. I saw it in his eyes even before I caught a faint whiff of it on his breath. Maybe it should have bothered me more. Maybe some sort of alarm should have gone off in my head. But it didn't. It wasn't unreasonable for a man to celebrate the news that he was about to become a father.

I should have been wiser, I suppose. I should have seen beneath the surface. I should have done something, said something. Maybe if I had . . .

Hindsight seems so clear, doesn't it?

CHAPTER EIGHTEEN

Bees hummed from purple blossom to purple blossom in the alfalfa fields kissed by the summer sun. The air was sweet and rich on this Saturday morning.

Janelle stopped her car in the driveway and the two of us got out, then walked in silence toward the house. It seemed forlorn with its windows boarded over. I paused near the back porch, awash in memories—bittersweet memories of Andy and me . . . and of Gideon and me.

I'd come here as a bride, flush with love and youthful belief that nothing bad could happen to me. I had lived here as a widow, heartbroken, the possessor of shattered dreams. I had left here once again a bride, in love and filled with renewed hope for the future.

Feeling the threat of tears, I turned from the house and stared across the barnyard. Would I cry throughout my pregnancy? I seemed forever on the brink.

The barn looked strange, empty as it was. Chickens should have been moving about the pen in a staccato rhythm—jerk and peck, jerk and peck. Daniel and Boone should have been in the corral, tails waving at pesky flies. Heidi should have been prancing along beside me or bouncing across the fields in the pursuit of squirrels and birds.

I hadn't visited the farm in six months. On an impulse, I'd asked Janelle if she would bring me here. I hadn't wanted to ask Gideon, and besides, he worked on Saturdays. Now I almost wished I hadn't come. I knew I needed to reach a difficult decision about this property. It was time to sell it. Everyone was right. What were the odds we would ever make our home here again? Our lives were in Boise. I needed to be practical.

As if reading my thoughts, Janelle asked, "Would you live here if it weren't such a commute into Boise?"

"Yes," I answered without hesitation.

"A farm's a good place to raise children."

I looked at her.

"I was raised on a farm," she said.

"I didn't know that."

Janelle nodded. "Over in Oregon. My father was a dairy farmer. He had an apple orchard, too. My brothers and sisters and I thinned apples for a dime a day." She smiled. "We used to accuse our parents of having lots of kids just so they could have cheap labor."

"Tell me again how many of you there are. I've forgotten."

"Ten. A baseball team and a spare. That's what Father called us."

We sat on the porch steps.

Janelle hooked a loose strand of auburn hair behind an ear.

"Some people would say we were a wild bunch of hoodlums when we were youngsters, but I wouldn't change a thing about us or the way we were raised."

"I'm envious when people tell stories about their brothers and sisters."

We'd talked about this before. Janelle knew I was an only child, and I knew she was third from the youngest in a large family. I also knew she wanted children but wasn't able to have them. Four times she'd miscarried, and the doctors had warned her against a fifth attempt.

"Don't kid yourself." Janelle laughed softly, intruding on my thoughts. "There are plenty of downsides to having that many siblings. More chances for things to go wrong, for one." Her smile faded. "I guess the worst for my family was when my youngest brother was sent to prison."

My eyes widened in surprise. This was a story I hadn't heard. "Whatever for?"

"When he was nineteen, Willie got into a barroom brawl. Punches were thrown. Bottles were broken." She drew a deep breath and let it out slowly. "A man died, and it was Willie's fault. He didn't mean to kill anybody, of course, but that's what happened."

Softly, I asked, "Is he still in prison?"

She nodded, then turned her head, gazing into the distance. "It was partly what happened to Willie that brought me to Christ. I was at such a low point, so heartbroken for my baby brother. Over the years, I tried to help him. He started drinking heavily when he was only fourteen, and it got him into all sorts of scrapes. I could see he was headed for real trouble, but he never listened to a thing I said. When he went to prison . . . " She swallowed hard.

I could tell she was fighting tears. For that matter, I was almost crying again myself.

"I don't know how anyone makes it without Jesus," Janelle finished in a whisper.

I knew what she said was true. I believed it. I believed Him. Yet I couldn't say so. I had no right to say anything. Not the way things stood between me and God. He felt far away. So very far. How had I moved so far away from Him?

Again, Janelle read my thoughts. "He's still with you, Deborah."

"I know." I rose from the porch step and strode toward the fields, distancing myself from my friend . . . and from the gentle, divine tug on my heart.

But God, it seemed, wouldn't be so easily ignored.

I'd walked no more than ten yards when I heard the crunch of gravel on the driveway. I turned to see a black Chevrolet roll to a stop beside Janelle's car. I raised my right hand to shield my eyes from the sun in time to observe Clyde Beekman step from the vehicle.

"Hello!" he called in a cheerful voice.

I waved, even as guilt tumbled in my stomach. Then I returned to the back porch.

"My goodness," Pastor Clyde said as he closed the distance between us. "If you aren't a sight for sore eyes. I wondered whose car that might be, but I never expected it to be you."

"Hello, Pastor."

He cast a quick glance around the barnyard. "Is your husband with you?"

"No, my friend drove me out."

"Ah." His gaze went to Janelle, who was now standing.

"This is Janelle Burns. We work together."

"A pleasure to meet you." Pastor Clyde offered Janelle his hand.

I finished the introduction. "Janelle, this is Pastor Beekman."

"Nice to meet you, sir." She took his hand and shook it.

Pastor Clyde looked at me again. "Dare I hope this means you'll be returning to Amethyst, Deborah? We've missed having you as part of our congregation."

"No. I'm afraid that's not what it means. I just . . . I just wanted to see the farm again. It's been a long time since I've been out here."

The pastor watched me with one of his calm but searching gazes. Internally I squirmed, fearful he would see something I didn't want him to see.

I decided to change the subject. "Gideon and I are expecting a baby early next year."

"Really? Well, praise the Lord!" He grasped my right hand within both of his. "May God watch over you and the baby. And Gideon."

"Thank you."

"Give Gideon my congratulations. In fact, I'd love to say the words to him myself. You should both come visit us at church. I know it's a bit of a drive, but one Sunday wouldn't be too much. The ladies would love a chance to give a baby shower in your honor."

"That would be nice, Pastor. I . . . I'll tell Gideon what you said."

As we exchanged a few more pleasantries, I wondered if I'd lied to the pastor. Would I tell Gideon about this visit? And if I did and Gideon agreed to it, would I want to visit Amethyst Community Church, being the spiritual imposter that I knew I was?

Vera Beekman

I scolded Clyde, something I try never to do. Try and all too often fail. I'm well aware what the Bible has to say about harping, contentious wives. We can be the dripping water torture that drive men mad. But sometimes my old nature gets the best of me, and this was one of those times.

Clyde came home from making some calls on his parishioners and told me he saw Deborah and that she was expecting a baby. Then he said he'd encouraged her to come visit us at church some Sunday.

That was what upset me. It wasn't, after all, Deborah's duty to come visit us. It was ours to visit her. Clyde was the pastor, the shepherd. But had we done that, visited her, even once since she and Gideon moved to Boise? No, we had not, and shame on us. Shame on us.

"Don't express concern for the sheep if you won't follow it with action," I chastised. "What use is your faith, Clyde, if you don't prove it by your actions? That kind of faith won't save anyone."

Oh, I know. Tossing the words of James at him was a shameless thing to do, and I would have to ask his—and the Lord's—forgiveness.

I suppose it was my own guilt that caused me to behave so. I know how to drive. I could have gone into Boise without Clyde months ago. I could have paid a visit on Deborah and Gideon, but I hadn't done it.

Shame on me.

CHAPTER NINETEEN

I didn't tell Gideon about my visit to the farm. I didn't tell him I'd seen Pastor Clyde, didn't relay the minister's invitation to visit them in Amethyst. I'd debated within myself whether I should tell him or not, but in the end, it wasn't up to me.

Gideon arrived home late again, complained of an upset stomach, saying he thought he had the flu, and went straight to bed. I was left alone all evening, me and my troubled thoughts. I awakened long before sunup on Sunday morning, still feeling restless and uneasy . . . and unhappy.

O God . . .

I loved my husband, and he loved me in return.

We were expecting a baby, a baby we both wanted and would love with our whole hearts.

We both had good jobs; I liked the people with whom I worked every day.

With the farm mortgage paid, we were debt free. We'd even opened a savings account and put money into it every payday.

And yet I was unhappy.

O God, You're so far away.

Only He wasn't far away. I knew that, deep down inside.

In my heart, I heard Janelle saying, *"He's still with you, Deborah."*

I slipped out of bed and went into the living room, Heidi right behind me. In the kitchenette, I stood at the sink and stared out the window. The alley was bathed in the soft white light of a full moon. The night was absolutely still. Not a breeze. Not a sound.

Across the way, a large black-and-white cat trotted along the thin-edged top of the neighbor's wooden fence, its tail held high. As a teenager, I'd had a cat that looked similar to the one on the fence. "Trouble," I'd christened him, and the name had fit him to a T. I smiled, a bit sadly, at the memory. How I'd loved that cat. He'd been a gift from my best friend the summer before our junior year of high school. She'd given him to me the week before I left for church camp.

I closed my eyes, remembering that camp and all it had meant to me, remembering especially the Wednesday evening when I'd given my heart to Jesus. Unlike Janelle's experience with her brother, there hadn't been a traumatic event that brought about my confession of faith. No, for me it had been a gentle but steady wooing, culminating in that night near the campfire when I'd known I needed Jesus Christ as my Savior and Lord of my life, a moment when I'd felt His love pour over and through me.

I stayed close to You in the beginning, Jesus. How did I end up so far from You now? When did I stop listening for the sound of Your voice?

My cheeks were damp with tears, but I didn't bother to wipe them dry.

Lord, why did I lose my first love? What caused me to grow cold? Help me, Jesus.

I didn't expect Him to answer. Why should He? After all, I'd ignored Him for the past year.

———

Four hours later, I slipped into the back pew of Grace Chapel, the church we'd visited two months earlier. I arrived late so I wouldn't need to make small talk with strangers. I didn't want to talk to anyone, no matter how welcoming they might be.

When the congregation rose to sing, I stood, too, holding a hymnal in both hands. But the words and notes on the page blurred before my eyes.

O Jesus . . . how do I find my way home?

I knew the story of the prodigal son. I knew he was welcomed with open arms by the father he'd left behind. But the prodigal had been a foolish rich boy who'd known no better. I, on the other hand—

Help me.

Coherent thought escaped me. My mind was filled with scraps of information, glimpses of shadowy images, fleeting memories. But nothing made sense. There was nothing I could grasp and hold on to. There was nothing that answered my silent pleas.

After the hymn ended and I was seated again, I reached for the Bible I'd brought to church with me and placed it on my lap. I ran the palm of my hand over the fine grain of the black leather cover.

O Father . . . I was so hungry for Your Word once. I couldn't get enough of it. Please give me a hunger for it again. I'm starving. Why don't I eat?

I opened the Bible and thumbed through the pages, my gaze sliding over words, not remaining long enough to comprehend what the passages said. Not until I saw a notation in the margin in Andy's familiar script.

Beside the underlined verse of Matthew 26:33—<u>Peter declared, "Even if everyone else deserts you, I never will."</u>— Andy had written,

See note in back.

Andy's Bible. I hadn't realized I'd taken his instead of my own. Probably because mine hadn't been opened in so long, another unused book on the shelf collecting dust.

I'm sorry, God.

I flipped to the back of the Bible, needing to see what Andy had written. I discovered many dated notes on the dozen or so once-blank pages that were there. I searched for the one relating to Matthew 26:33 and found it on the fourth page.

The strength of pride lasts only for a moment. Peter's love for the Lord was true, ardent, and sincere, but he relied too much on his own strength rather than on God's.

If Peter's declaration had been one of humble dependence upon God's grace and strength, it would have been an excellent promise. But it wasn't spoken in humility. A victim of his own arrogance, he went on to deny the Lord three times.

I've seen this happen in my life. I'm so sure of myself, so arrogant and proud, so convinced I won't sin in a certain way. Then that's

exactly the way in which I sin. By my thoughts and by my actions, I've denied Christ once, twice, thrice.

I've got two choices any time I sin, any time I take the wrong path, any time I fail to live a triumphant Christian life. I can stay in sin, sometimes wallowing in guilt but not doing anything about the cause itself, or I can learn from the experience and ask the Lord to help me overcome my weaknesses.

It's at times like those, times when I've stumbled and fallen, when I've been trapped by my sins, and then at last turn to God for His help and forgiveness, that I discover anew the unending love and mercy of Jesus, those moments when I hear Him whisper, as He did to Peter in John 21, "Andy, do you love Me?" And even though (like Peter) my heart is grieved that He's had to ask me once again, I can respond (again like Peter), "Yes, Lord, You know I love You."

When I do that, when I respond to Him, I feel Him lift the cloud of my denial. I feel Him restore me so that I, in turn, might reach out to others.

Yes, Lord, You know I love You. Teach me to show that love to the world so others may know You, too.

I read Andy's lengthy note, then went back to the beginning and read it again. I tried to remember the man who, on this page, had called himself arrogant and proud. I tried to imagine him stumbling and falling in his faith. But I couldn't. That wasn't the man I'd known. The Andy I remembered had been so rock solid, so steady, so humble and dependent upon God. The Andy I remembered had shown his love for Christ to others in countless ways.

And yet, this entry implied there'd been times when he wavered, times when he sinned, times when he had to repent and return to God.

I heard His voice then. I heard the Lord as clearly as if He were seated next to me on the pew: *Beloved, do you love Me?*

My heart hammered. My breath caught in my chest. My eyes misted.

Deborah, my daughter, do you love Me?

I swallowed the lump in my throat. *Yes, Lord, I love You. You know I love You.*

Is it possible to *feel* God smile? It must be, for I'm sure I did. His smile fell upon me like a ray of sunshine, warm and bright and all-encompassing.

Amazing grace! How sweet the sound—the old and beloved hymn welled in my heart—*that saved a wretch like me! I once was lost, but now am found; was blind, but now I see.*

So great was the joy that washed through me! It was all I could do not to stand and start singing at the top of my lungs.

─────

I rushed home, eager to share with Gideon what had happened to me at church.

"Where've you been?" he asked as I entered the house a short while later.

Gideon stood at the stove, eggs frying in the skillet. His eyes were filled with slumber, and I knew he wasn't long out of bed.

"At church. I left you a note." I glanced at the small table near the door where we left notes to each other. The slip of paper was in plain view.

Gideon raked his fingers through his disheveled hair as he yawned. "Sorry. I didn't think to look for a note. Guess my head's not on straight yet."

"Are you feeling better?" I went to him and kissed his cheek.

"I think so." He turned back to his eggs. "I'll know better

once I get something in my stomach. Want to join me? I made plenty."

I wasn't hungry, but I said, "Okay," as I set Andy's Bible and my pocketbook on the dinette table.

"Thanks for not waking me up, by the way. I really needed to sleep."

"I could tell." I took a deep breath, mentally searching for the best way to begin. I wanted him to know all that I was feeling—the joy, the peace, the wonder.

Gideon took a couple of plates from the cupboard. "What church did you visit this time?"

Hopeful this was the opening I needed, I answered, "I went back to Grace Chapel."

"The one with the grouchy minister?"

"He wasn't grouchy, Gideon."

"No? Sure seemed like it to me."

I suppressed a sigh. "I enjoyed today's service."

Gideon dismissed my comment with a grunt as he scooped scrambled eggs, fried with chopped peppers and bits of bacon, onto the plates. "Grab the juice, will you?" He moved past me, plates in hand.

Obediently, I took the pitcher of orange juice from the refrigerator and carried it to the table. Before sitting down, I filled both of the glasses on the table.

"Thanks." Gideon added ketchup to his eggs and began to eat.

I picked up my fork, then set it down again and closed my eyes. *Thank You, Lord, for this food. Thank You for Your grace, which You poured out on me this morning. Help me find the words to share with Gideon what You've shown me. He's stumbling around apart from You, just as I've been doing for too long. I want us to find our way back together. In Jesus' name, Amen.*

I opened my eyes and found Gideon observing me with what could only be called an annoyed gaze.

"Don't ask me to go back to that church with you, Deb, 'cause I won't."

"But—"

"Don't even ask."

"All right. I won't ask you to go with me." I took a deep breath. "But tell me this. Why did you stop wanting to go to church in the first place?" I lifted a hand before he could utter a word of protest. "I'm trying to understand the same thing about myself, but I want to know about you, too."

He shoved his plate away from the edge of the table. "You're not going to get all super-religious on me, are you?"

"You accepted Christ in Korea. Andy told me. You loved Jesus. You told me that yourself when you first started coming out to the farm." I paused to swallow the lump in my throat. "What happened to your relationship with Jesus, Gideon?"

He rose so abruptly his chair tipped over backward. "I'm not Andy, and I'm never going to be."

The heat of Gideon's anger—an anger made worse because I hadn't anticipated it—hit me like a slap in the face.

"I'll never be perfect the way he was."

"Gideon, Andy wasn't—"

"Wasn't he? You always talk about him as if he was."

"That isn't true. And it isn't fair."

"Life isn't fair, Deb. You of all people should know that."

Bernice Richardson

When I called Deborah that Sunday afternoon, I could tell she'd been crying. She tried to pass it off as stuffiness from a head cold, but I knew better. A mother has a certain instinct pertaining to her children.

The reason for my call was her birthday, which was only three days away. Henry and I planned to take Deborah and Gideon to dinner at a nice restaurant in downtown Boise. I wanted to confirm the time of our reservation with her.

Deborah showed no interest whatsoever.

I tried to get her to open up, but my daughter can be terribly stubborn when she wants to be. She continued to insist nothing was wrong other than having the sniffles.

"I hate summer colds," she said. "They seem worse than winter ones. Don't you think?"

Why I don't save my breath when she gets like that, heaven only knows. I can't think of a single time when I've managed to change her mind, despite all of my best efforts.

Well, I'll tell you this. I had no intention of leaving it be. Deborah was unhappy about something, and I meant to find out what.

CHAPTER TWENTY

Gideon apologized later for making me cry. He even listened as I haltingly tried to tell him what I'd felt God doing in my heart. And yet things weren't okay between us. Not really. They wouldn't be as long as Gideon felt he was living in my first husband's shadow. I understood that, but I didn't know how to change it.

Perhaps because he was right. Perhaps I had made Andy perfect in my mind and heart. And I couldn't deny that I still loved my first husband—or at least, the memory of him.

But was love a commodity that must be measured? Did a person only have a capacity for so much love and not an ounce more? Wasn't it possible for me to love the Andy of my memories and still love Gideon with my whole heart?

On Wednesday morning—my thirty-second birthday—I opened my eyes to find a small box, wrapped in bright yellow tissue paper, on the nightstand beside the bed.

Gideon was nowhere to be seen.

I sat up, pushed my unruly hair away from my face with both hands, then reached for the gift. I smiled, wondering what was inside but hating to open it and end the suspense.

Oh, Gideon. Thanks. I love you.

As if summoned by my thoughts, Gideon appeared in the bedroom doorway. "Morning, my beautiful wife."

There was a tenderness in his eyes that I hadn't seen in a while. It made my heart skip a beat as he came to sit on the side of the bed next to me.

"Aren't you going to open that?" he asked.

"I was savoring it."

"Silly girl." He leaned close and kissed me on the forehead. "The box isn't the gift. You need to open it and see what's inside."

"I know."

"Happy birthday." He brushed my lips with his. "I love you, Deborah Clermont."

"I love you, too," I whispered.

"Now open the package, will you?"

I laughed as I lifted the tape from both ends, then removed the yellow paper. Inside was a jewelry box. Even wrapped I had suspected that much. I opened the lid.

Nestled against the black velvet interior was a sterling silver pendant. In the center was a small pearl. A bloodred stone dangled beneath it.

"It's beautiful," I said, raising my eyes to Gideon.

"They told me at the jeweler's that a garnet's the birthstone for January, when the baby's due. And the cultured pearl is your birthstone."

"Oh, Gideon." Of course, my eyes teared. "That's so thoughtful."

He drew me close, cheek against cheek, and whispered in my ear, "Eventually, I hope we can add several more pendants to the chain. Maybe you can have a whole rainbow of different birthstones."

I laughed softly. "Don't be in such a rush. We haven't been introduced to our January baby yet."

— *Janelle Burns* —

If I live to be a hundred, I'll never forget the look of stark terror on Deborah's face when she called me into her office.

"I need you to take me to the hospital," she said. "I . . . I'm bleeding."

On our way out the door, I told someone—I don't remember who—to get word to Gideon at the construction site. "Tell him he needs to meet us at St. Luke's."

I hate hospitals. I get dizzy whenever I go to visit someone there. I don't know if it's the antiseptic smell or the sterile whiteness of everything or maybe it's a deep-seated fear of illness, one I'm not even conscious of. I only know I've been this way since I was a child.

Within moments of our arrival at the emergency ward, the nurses whisked Deborah away. I was left to pace the waiting room, anxious for word about Deborah and her baby, anxious for Gideon to arrive so he could be with her.

I prayed while I paced. I prayed Deborah wouldn't

miscarry. I prayed her baby would be healthy and whole. I prayed Deborah's faith, just beginning to blossom anew, wouldn't be shaken, no matter what happened. I prayed . . . and then I trusted the Father to accomplish His will.

CHAPTER TWENTY-ONE

The emergency room was a nightmare.

The doctor on call and several nurses came and went. They poked and prodded, asked questions but answered none, told me to lie on my left side and stay there but didn't say why, started an IV and drew my blood. Beyond the curtained exam area, people spouted numbers and tossed around medical terms I'd heard of before but didn't understand.

I wanted my husband. I wanted some answers. I wanted the bleeding and the pain to cease.

God, please don't let me lose the baby. Please let Gideon get here. Please, please, please.

I closed my eyes, bargaining with God, promising to be a better wife, a better mother, a better Christian if only I wouldn't lose our baby.

"Deb?"

I opened my eyes to find Gideon standing beside the bed. "Honey?"

I started to sob as I pressed the back of his hand against my cheek. With his free hand, Gideon stroked my hair.

"Excuse me," a nurse said from the opening in the curtains. "Are you Mr. Clermont?"

"Yes, I am," he answered. "What—"

"If you'd like to step out to the nurse's station, we need some information from you."

I clutched his hand tighter.

The nurse met my panicked gaze and gave me a gentle smile. "It's okay, dear. I won't take him far or keep him long. I promise."

I tried to loosen my grasp, but my fingers wouldn't obey. Gideon leaned over and kissed my forehead. "I'll be right back."

"They haven't told me anything," I whispered. "Make them tell you what's happening." *Make them tell you I won't lose this baby.*

He nodded, and I wondered if he'd read my mind as well as heard my words. Then he slipped his hand from mine and disappeared beyond the curtains, leaving me alone.

Muffled footsteps hurried from one place to another. The sounds seemed otherworldly.

God, I don't think I could bear losing our baby. Please let this child be all right. Please, Father.

It was an agonizing wait until Gideon returned, although I suppose he was gone no more than ten or fifteen minutes.

"What did they say?" I asked the instant he appeared.

He shook his head.

Before I could press him for information, both the doctor I'd seen earlier and the nurse with the gentle smile who'd taken Gideon away entered the examination area.

"Mr. Clermont, I'm Dr. Miller." He shook hands with Gideon. "I'm attending Dr. Ogilvie's patients while he's out of town." He opened the chart and studied the notations inside before meeting my gaze.

"Am I going to lose the baby?"

"You appear to have a subchorionic hematoma. While your body has threatened to miscarry, your cervix is closed. That's a good sign." He glanced at the chart again. "You and your husband are both Rh-positive. That's good news, too." He looked up. "We'll know more in the next twenty-four hours. We'd like to keep you overnight for observation, Mrs. Clermont."

Such simple words, yet so ominous sounding.

"We'll get you settled into a room for now, and I'll be back to see you later in the day." He handed the chart to the nurse. Then he patted my shin, covered with a soft flannel blanket. "Don't worry, Mrs. Clermont."

Don't worry? How easily he spoke those words. It wasn't his baby in jeopardy.

O God, please . . .

The doctor thought it better that I not have other visitors, including my parents, but Gideon was allowed to stay with me for the remainder of the afternoon and early evening. However, he was so agitated it was almost a relief when he kissed me good night and told me he would see me in the morning.

"Pray for the baby," I told him before he could move away from the bed.

He nodded. "I will."

"I love you, Gideon."

"I love you, too." He kissed me a second time. "Don't worry. You're going to be okay. So's the baby."

It was my turn to nod.

I don't know if either of us believed it.

Gideon gave my shoulder a gentle squeeze; then he turned and left, drawing the door closed behind him.

The solitude was not nearly as comforting as I'd hoped it would be. The sterile walls closed in around me. I reached for a magazine on the stand beside my hospital bed. I flipped through the pages, finding nothing to hold my interest.

Janelle had offered to go to my house and bring some of my personal items to me, but I'd told her it wasn't necessary. I was only here overnight. Now I wished I'd said yes.

I longed to get up and walk around a bit, but I'd been given strict instructions to remain in bed.

With a sigh, I looked to see what other magazines had been left on the stand. There was nothing I cared to read, so I pulled open the drawer. Inside was a Gideon Bible. I reached for it, then closed the drawer again. I didn't open the Bible immediately. It seemed enough to hold it in my hands.

As I allowed my eyes to drift closed, I heard a long-familiar passage of Scripture echo in my heart: *Keep on asking, and you will be given what you ask for. Keep on looking, and you will find. Keep on knocking, and the door will be opened. For everyone who asks, receives. Everyone who seeks, finds. And the door is opened to everyone who knocks.*

"Father God," I whispered, "I'm asking. I'm looking for Your answers. I'm knocking on Your door. Keep my baby safe. Allow me to carry this child to term. Help me to raise this baby to know You and to love You from childhood onward."

I knew then. I believed it with my whole heart. My baby would be all right.

Still holding the Bible to my chest, I drifted off to sleep.

— *Jack Clermont* —

My brother was drunk when he called me.

It was after midnight, and the jangling telephone jerked me out of a sound sleep. It took me a moment or two to come fully awake, a little bit longer to understand what Gideon was trying to tell me.

Deborah was in the hospital and they were afraid she might lose the baby.

I told him to get a grip on himself. I told him his wife needed him to be strong. "Getting drunk isn't going to help Deborah or your baby."

I don't know if he heard me or understood what I was saying. He just kept talking, his speech slow, his words slurred, and I got madder and madder the longer I listened to him.

Everything always went wrong for him, he told me. Why couldn't something go right for a change? The only sort of luck he had was bad luck. What did he do to deserve this?

Finally, I'd had enough. "What about all that religious stuff you were spouting when you came back from Korea? I thought Christianity was supposed to change you, Gideon."

"But you don't understand."

"Grow up, man," I snapped.

And then I hung up the phone.

CHAPTER TWENTY-TWO

I was discharged from the hospital the next morning with strict instructions for complete bed rest for the next week, perhaps longer if the spotting didn't completely subside by then. Mother volunteered to stay with me during the daytime hours so Gideon wouldn't have to miss more work.

"I can take a few days off if you want me to," he said during the drive home. "The boss'll understand."

"No, honey. That's okay. I'll be fine with Mother. She'll love fussing over me. Besides, I know you're in the middle of a big job."

Gideon grunted. I assumed it was a sound of agreement.

I glanced at him. His forehead was pinched with a frown, and he looked dreadfully tired, deep circles etching half-moons beneath his eyes. His jaw was dark with stubble, evidence that he hadn't taken time to shave. He looked worse than I felt.

He's worried. About me and the baby. About all the medical bills, too.

I turned my head to gaze out the window at the passing neighborhood.

"Your mother's already here," Gideon said as he turned the corner.

Sure enough, Mother stood on the sidewalk, her green Nash parked near the alley. Heidi waited right beside her, as if she understood I was coming home.

When Mother saw us, she lifted her hand in a wave. She wore a big smile, but she didn't fool me for an instant. She was as worried as Gideon. She would be an unrelenting nurse during my convalescence.

Gideon pulled the truck to the curb behind my mother's car. Before I could reach for the handle, Mother had the passenger door open.

"Don't you move an inch, young lady," she ordered. "Gideon will carry you into the house."

"Mother, I can walk."

"The doctor said bed rest, and I'm here to see you obey his orders."

"Yes, ma'am." I looked to my left. Lowering my voice, I said, "Darling, I think we'd better do exactly as she says. Or else."

In that moment, the frown on his forehead eased, and he gave me one of his special smiles, a silent communication for me and me alone, a look that never failed to make me feel cherished. With his gaze, he told me we were going to be fine, that not even being ordered about by my mother was going to disturb either one of us.

To my surprise, I realized I wasn't going to mind being pampered for a few days. I knew, as irritating as it could be at times, that this was one way my mother showed her love for me.

Little baby— I placed the flat of my hand on my abdomen—
I promise to be a good mother to you. I promise to take all of my
mother's best qualities and then add the ones God gives me. I promise
to raise you up in the ways of the Lord. I promise to try to make wise
choices, and I promise to bathe your life in prayer.

I slept for a few hours after Gideon left for work, and when
I awakened, the bedroom was filled with the warm scents of
cinnamon and nutmeg. Mother was baking sugar cookies. My
favorite.

As if sensing I was awake—although I suspected she'd looked
in on me about every five minutes throughout my nap—Mother
cracked open the door to my room.

I pushed myself upright on the bed. "I'm awake."

"Did you rest well, dear?"

I nodded.

"Can I get you anything? How about a glass of iced tea?
It's nice and cold."

"Maybe in a little while. Right now, I'd like to use the bathroom." I pushed aside the sheet and sat on the side of the bed.

"Deborah, you let me help you." She hurried forward.

"I can walk, Mother. Really. I went to the bathroom on
my own in the hospital."

"Well, bully for you."

Her stubborn—and unexpected—retort made me laugh
out loud.

"Laugh all you want, Deborah Clermont, but I *will* help you
to and from the bathroom."

Still smiling, I shook my head as I said, "I love you, Mother.
You're the best."

A rosy hue infused her cheeks, and she sputtered something about me not being ridiculous. Then she slipped her arms beneath mine and helped me up from the bed.

I promised myself that, in the future, I would be better about telling my mother I loved her.

The trek to the bathroom was made without mishap, and I was soon ensconced once again in my bed, pillows fluffed at my back, a tall glass of iced tea, along with two still-warm sugar cookies, on the bed tray beside me, and a novel resting on my lap. Mother returned to the kitchen to begin dinner preparations. I heard cupboards opening and closing and the rattle of pots and pans as she searched for the things she needed.

A few days of Mother's cooking and Gideon might never be satisfied with my cooking again. I bit into a cookie. *A few days of her cooking, and I might never be satisfied with mine again.*

I grinned, opened the book, and began to read.

— Norman Adams —

No getting around it. Gideon looked like a train wreck when he showed up at work around noon, right after taking his wife home from the hospital.

Me and the rest of the crew were worried about him, but he'd been grumpy and out of sorts so much of the time nobody wanted to say anything. We all felt bad, of course. We knew he'd been looking forward to being a dad.

I couldn't help wondering if more was wrong than the obvious. Maybe his marriage was on the rocks. After all, he'd felt like he was competing with a dead man. He'd said so—or words to that effect—that one time. Maybe he couldn't handle it anymore. I supposed it was possible to want to be a dad even while being miserable as a husband.

But when I remembered how Gideon and Deborah acted with each other the day they got married in Winnemucca, I couldn't believe there was anything too seriously wrong between them.

It had to be just his worries about the baby. Had to be.

CHAPTER TWENTY-THREE

The novel I'd chosen hadn't been an edifying read by any stretch of the imagination, but it had helped pass the time. So had the stack of magazines Mother brought over and the small-sized jigsaw puzzle Dad gave me.

By Saturday afternoon, however, after three days abed, I was feeling more than a little impatient with my captivity. The cramping had subsided, and the spotting had lessened as well. I believed I was over the worst danger, and I wanted to get up for short periods of time.

Mother—my unrelenting, self-appointed jailer—wouldn't hear of it. "You will stay in that bed for the full week, Deborah, just as the doctor told you."

"But all I want to do is sit on the couch for a few hours. That can't hurt. It would be nice to watch some television to help pass the time."

"Dr. Miller said bed rest."

"Mother, really."

"Don't 'Mother, really' me. I'm not about to let you risk your health or the well-being of that baby so you can watch some ridiculous show."

Then I'll wait until Gideon gets home. He'll let me get out of bed.

Mother shook her finger at me, as if I were four years old instead of thirty-two. "I know what's going on in that head of yours, young lady. Don't think I don't. I'll have a word or two with Gideon before I leave."

I released a dramatic sigh as I sank against the pillows and closed my eyes.

Mother sighed, too—every bit as dramatically as I. Then she left the bedroom.

Oh, she was being so unreasonable, so difficult, so bossy, so interfering. I couldn't help being irritated with her when she insisted on treating me like a child. She needed to let me live my own life. She needed to keep her nose out of—

I drew myself up short, realizing that my *thoughts* about Mother should be as respectful as my words should be. Convicted, I prayed: *Father, forgive me. I know a gentle answer turns away wrath. Help me to be gentle with Mother, to show her how much I love her.*

Thirty-two years ago, my mother had been like me, a young woman expecting a baby, wanting to be a good parent, promising to do the very best she could by her child.

I laid a hand on my flat abdomen, silently acknowledging what a wonderful childhood I'd had. There'd never been a time when I hadn't known I was loved and cherished. There hadn't been a school play or a music lesson or a dance rehearsal that my mother missed. Raising a child in the midst of the

Great Depression couldn't have been easy, but I had been blissfully unaware of whatever struggles my parents had gone through.

I felt like crying, but I had something I needed to do first. "Mother, could you come here, please?"

Moments later, she appeared in my bedroom doorway.

"Mother, I'm sorry."

"Deborah, what's wrong?" She hurried toward me, concern in her eyes.

"I didn't mean to argue with you. When I came home from the hospital, I promised myself I wouldn't be difficult and ungrateful, but that's exactly what I've been." I wiped my nose with a handkerchief. "I'm so ashamed of myself. You're a wonderful mother. You've poured yourself out for me all my life, and I'm an ungrateful wretch."

"Oh, sweetie. You don't need to cry. You aren't an ungrateful wretch. You're a wonderful daughter. You're just restless, that's all. I know it's hard to be stuck in bed for so long." She sat beside me and took hold of one of my hands. "Goodness, dear. It really is no reason to cry."

"I . . . I love . . . you." This was going to turn into a full-fledged crying jag. I could feel it coming.

Mother gathered me into her arms and stroked my hair with the palm of her hand and crooned to me like the child I was. "You go right ahead and cry, honey. Everything's going to be all right."

———

Neither of us knew how wrong she was. Neither of us knew how wrong things could go. Neither of us perceived the storm that was barreling toward me with great ferocity.

If I'd known, what would I have done? Would it have changed anything?

Clyde Beekman

It was late on a Saturday afternoon when Vera and I dropped in to see Deborah. Her mother showed us into the bedroom, then returned to the kitchen to make a pot of coffee, even though we insisted it wasn't necessary.

My wife immediately launched into the usual feminine noises about what an adorable apartment the converted garage was, and wasn't it cozy and quaint. Personally, I found it claustrophobic—and I'm not a man given to phobias.

When I was able to get a word in edgewise, I asked about Deborah's health. She was quick to inform me she was doing well. "And I finally found a church, Pastor Clyde."

I could tell that her comment was about far more than attendance of services on Sunday mornings. There was an unmistakable light in her eyes that had been missing for too long.

Thank You, Jesus.

Deborah placed a hand on her stomach. "I feel like God told me the baby is going to be fine. Does that sound like wishful thinking on my part?"

"God speaks to us in many ways," I answered. "I can't tell you what He may or may not have said to you, Deborah, but I know He answers our prayers."

CHAPTER TWENTY-FOUR

I asked Gideon to take me to church the next morning—how much could it hurt me or the baby to sit in a pew for one hour?—but he was every bit as stubborn as Mother when it came to that suggestion.

However, as it was a beautiful day, he agreed to let me go outside to sit in the shade of the tall maple tree. He carried me to the lounger, treating me as if I were a complete invalid. I didn't object. It was lovely to be held in his arms.

As if he'd read my thoughts, he leaned over the lounge chair and kissed me on the lips, the slow kind of kiss that made my toes curl, as the saying goes. When he drew back, he asked, "How about I go to the store and get a couple of steaks to put on the barbecue?"

"Mmm. Sounds good." I glanced toward our landlady's house. "We should ask Mr. and Mrs. Andrus to join us. They've been so kind to us."

The closing of a car door drew our attention to the street. There was Janelle and her husband, Ted, both dressed in their Sunday best. Janelle held a potted plant.

She waved when she saw me on the lounger. "Hi! Hope you don't mind us dropping in like this."

"Ask your friends to stay," Gideon said softly. "I'll get six steaks at the store, and we'll make a party of it."

Moments later, Janelle and Ted entered the yard through the back gate.

"We come bearing a get-well gift." Janelle handed the plant to Gideon. Then she leaned over my chair to clasp one of my hands between both of hers. "You look wonderful today, Deborah. There's color in your cheeks again. Gideon is obviously taking good care of you."

"He is."

"I'm trying," Gideon interjected, "but she isn't an easy patient. Stubborn. Just like her mother."

I gave him a warning glance, one weakened by my subsequent smile. Returning my gaze to Janelle, I said, "Gideon's going to barbecue steaks. Can you and Ted join us for lunch?"

"Well, we—"

"Please. We'd really like you to."

Janelle and Ted looked at each other; then she nodded. "All right, but we'll want to help. What can we do?"

Gideon patted my shoulder. "You can pull up a lawn chair and visit with Deb while I make a quick run to the store. And make sure she doesn't get off that lounger for any reason. Sit on her if you have to."

"I can do that," Janelle answered.

"Want me to get the charcoal going in the grill?" Ted asked my husband.

"Sure. That would be great." Gideon gave my shoulder another pat. "Be back in a jiff."

———

It turned out to be an absolutely perfect afternoon. The temperature rose to the upper eighties, but in the leafy shade of the backyard trees, it was pleasant, a gentle breeze stirring the air.

Ted stood with Gideon near the grill as the steaks cooked. Janelle, Clarice Andrus, and her husband, Robert, sat with me, sipping lemonade while we discussed everything from President Eisenhower's recent surgery for some intestinal disease, to the segregationist riots in Alabama the previous winter, to the nuclear testing going on in Nevada, to the lives and loves of such notables as Rock Hudson, Princess Grace, and Elvis Presley.

When everything was ready, Gideon spread two blankets on the lawn, and Heidi was relegated to her kennel while we ate our Sunday dinner of grilled steaks, baked potatoes, and a fresh garden salad. For dessert, Mrs. Andrus contributed strawberry shortcake with whipped cream.

"If I take even one more bite, I won't be able to get off this lounger with the help of a crane." I set my plate on the grass beside me.

Janelle laughed. "I know what you mean. I'm stuffed to the gills." She turned toward Gideon. "You did the cooking. I'll do the dishes."

"Janelle, you don't have to—," I began.

"Yes, I do. I insist. We were visitors who dropped by unexpectedly, and you made us honored guests." She stood. "Where can I find an apron and the dish soap?"

I could tell there was no point in arguing with her, so I answered her question.

Ted stacked the dishes and serving bowls and carried them into the apartment while Gideon took the leftover dessert makings into Mrs. Andrus's kitchen. Soon I was all alone in the backyard. I closed my eyes, feeling full and contented.

A beautiful, warm summer day. A picnic beneath the trees. A congenial landlady. Good friends with whom I could laugh. A husband who loved me. And a baby who would join our family in January.

Thank You, Father.

"Need anything, hon?"

I opened my eyes again. Gideon stood at the foot of the lounger.

"No thanks."

"Okay. I'll finish putting things away."

I smiled and let my eyes drift closed a second time.

For some reason, I thought of the farm, of the sounds of the barnyard animals and fragrance of new-mown alfalfa. I remembered the coziness of the house and the sight of Heidi bounding through the fields.

The contentment I'd felt there, before Andy died, I now felt here.

Is it time, Lord? Is it time to sell the farm? Have I been holding something back that should have been given up? Help me know what I should do. If it's time to let go, make it clear to me, please.

Halfway between wakefulness and slumber, I imagined myself kneeling on the lawn beside the farmhouse, the golden rays of a dying day kissing the treetops and casting long shadows. A child in T-shirt and diapers toddled toward me with uncertain steps.

It seemed so real, that daydream. It was almost like a promise.

Janelle Burns

That Sunday of the barbecue was the first time I really got to know Gideon Clermont—our other meetings had been brief—and it was easy to see why Deborah loved him. He was completely charming.

I was happy for my friend.

CHAPTER TWENTY-FIVE

Dr. Ogilvie had been practicing medicine in Boise for more than thirty years. He'd seen me through a series of childhood illnesses and injuries, and I trusted him completely. While I'd liked Dr. Miller well enough, it was comforting to see the wizened face of my family physician on Monday morning.

Mother had offered to drive me so Gideon wouldn't have to miss work, but my husband had insisted on being with me. I was grateful for that.

After the doctor completed his examination, he asked Gideon and me to step into his office. I wasn't sure if that was a good sign or a bad one, and I felt my confidence slipping a bit as I settled onto one of the burgundy-colored leather-upholstered chairs.

Dr. Ogilvie began, "I'm sure my associate, Dr. Miller, was quite thorough in explaining the nature of a threatened miscarriage, but I'd like to cover it again, if that's all right."

I took hold of Gideon's hand as I nodded.

"A miscarriage is more likely to occur in the early months of pregnancy rather than later. The premature separation and expulsion of a fetus can be induced by numerous causes, both of a local and general nature, such as malformations of the pelvis, accidental injuries, and various conditions of the placenta, which can lead to the death of the fetus. If the latter is the case, there won't be any stopping the miscarriage."

My grip tightened on Gideon's hand. I think I stopped breathing.

"When a miscarriage is threatened, as happened in your case, the usual treatment consists of rest and the use of astringents and sedatives. That is the course I would like you to continue to follow in the coming weeks. Plenty of rest is of primary importance."

"I could still lose our baby?"

"It remains a possibility, Deborah."

O God, I thought we were past the danger. Was I wrong?

"But you needn't expect the worst to happen," the doctor continued in a reassuring tone. "The more time that goes by, the better the chances you will carry to term."

Gideon said, "You're saying Deborah needs to quit her job. Right?"

"Yes. I think that would be wise."

Gideon met my gaze. "Then that's what she'll do. We won't take any risks with her or the baby. She'll quit her job today."

I had no intention of arguing with him, but he didn't wait to see if I would.

"You would've quit work when the baby came anyway. This just means you'll be doing it a few months earlier. We don't need your income, Deb. I can provide for us."

"I know you can."

Dr. Ogilvie scribbled something on a prescription pad, then held the slip of paper toward Gideon. "Deborah should begin taking these today." To me, he said, "I want you to continue bed rest for the remainder of this week. After that, you may resume moderate activity as long as you don't experience cramping or observe increased spotting. But no heavy exertion and don't stay standing or walking for long periods. Take frequent breaks with your feet up. Understood?"

I nodded.

"Do either of you have any questions?"

All I truly wanted was to be told my baby would be all right, that I wouldn't lose him or her. But I knew the doctor wouldn't promise that.

"All right then. Make an appointment with my receptionist to see me again in two weeks. And try not to worry, Deborah. That isn't good for you either."

"I'll try."

Don't worry.

I silently repeated those words as I scheduled my next appointment.

Don't worry.

I repeated them as Gideon and I walked to the truck, parked near the corner of Second and Idaho Streets.

Don't worry. Don't worry.

I repeated them as we drove toward home.

Don't worry. Don't worry. Don't worry.

But I *was* worried. The doctor's words had shaken me. I'd been so certain I'd received God's promise while I was still in the hospital. And now . . . now I was afraid.

Arriving at our apartment, Gideon cut the truck's engine,

then turned toward me, a frown knitting his brows. "You know what the Bible says about worry, Deb? It says we shouldn't."

The look I gave him was filled with surprise.

"Even I know some Scriptures." He shrugged. "Now, let's get you inside and into bed. Your mother'll be here soon, and I'll catch what for if you're still up. Besides, you need to call your office to tender your resignation, and I need to get back to the job site."

⁓

Later that afternoon—after I called Edward Cooper, the managing partner at Cooper, Smith, and Peevey, to tell him I wouldn't be able to return to work and after I took a nap at Mother's behest—I went outside to the lounge chair. Seated beneath the shade trees, I spent over an hour with my Bible and a concordance, looking up verses about worrying and not worrying, about faith and not doubting, and about the power of prayer.

I'd known the written word of God had living power, that it was sharper than the sharpest knife, cutting deep into my innermost thoughts and desires, but that afternoon I experienced it afresh.

"Why do people forget so easily, Father?" I whispered. "The whole earth declares Your glory, yet we still forget."

I thought of the Israelites, of the many times recorded in Scripture when God rescued and restored them, of the many times they turned to Him with worship and praise, and of the many times they forgot His power and grace and returned to their old ways.

But I didn't want to be like that. Not again. I didn't want to be guilty of forsaking my first love, of allowing my devotion to the Lord to grow cold in my heart. I never wanted to walk that lonely road again.

"Jesus, make me a woman of strong faith. Keep me from doubt and fear. Help me to believe and not waver." I drew a long, deep breath. "No matter what happens, keep me steady in You."

Bernice Richardson

For heaven's sake, I knew I'd been guilty of hovering at times, of trying to shelter my daughter from the difficulties of life. I've always been overprotective of the people I love, but especially of Deborah. Perhaps it was because she's my only child. Or perhaps it was because she's known so much heartache in her thirty-two years. Widowed young. Now in danger of losing a child.

Why must motherhood be so difficult? I sometimes believe God gives us children not for the lessons we can teach them but more for the lessons they will teach us.

Do you suppose that's true?

At any rate, I was glad to be able to report to Henry that things were improving for our daughter. Deborah seemed in much improved spirits, and my observations of her and Gideon together convinced me things were well between them. After that day on the telephone when I thought she was crying, I hadn't been so sure. Now I was.

Deborah's father, dear soul, simply smiled and said I worry too much.

Well, now. Isn't that what I just told you? It's my nature.

CHAPTER TWENTY-SIX

The weather forecast on the Fourth of July was for temperatures near one hundred degrees with possible thunderstorms blowing through the valley by late afternoon.

After serving me breakfast in bed—I warned Gideon I could get used to that particular treatment—he said he was going to catch up on some chores, including changing the oil in the truck, before the weather turned ugly.

Left alone, I lingered over the morning newspaper, then took a shower. Afterward, clad in a terry-cloth bathrobe and rubbing my hair with a towel, I walked to the bedroom window that looked out onto the street. The front wheels of the truck were up on risers, and I could see Gideon's legs sticking out from beneath the cab.

He was a hard worker, my husband. He put in long hours on the job, six days a week, then spent much of his spare time keeping up with other projects around our apartment and our landlady's yard. Oh, I knew Gideon wasn't perfect. He had his moments of irritability, mostly in the mornings before he was completely awake; I'd learned in the eight months we'd been married that it was better not to ask him questions when he first got up. But overall I couldn't have asked for a better mate.

A swell of love washed over me, like an ocean wave breaking over a rocky shoreline. Overwhelmed by its power, I sank onto the edge of the bed, then lay back and stared at the ceiling. I crossed my arms over my chest, hugging myself even as I imagined I was hugging Gideon.

A year ago I was drowning in a sea of sorrow and despair. A year ago I believed my life was over. My heart had been broken, and I was alone. A year ago, I felt far, far from God.

Father, thank You for bringing Gideon into my life. Thank You for letting me love again. There's only one thing that could make our marriage better than it is, and that would be for Gideon to be strong in his faith again. I know he belongs to You, but I want us to worship You together. Draw him back into fellowship as You drew me back. Make him hungry for You and Your Word. Let our child grow up in a home that's filled with the knowledge of You. Let our child see the love of Christ in our marriage every single day.

Feeling emotional and close to tears, I sat up and swiped my eyes with the towel. Then I walked into the bathroom. Staring at my reflection in the mirror, I wondered if I should cut my hair short. I'd worn it the same way for years. It would be easier to care for. Or would it? Hmm. I'd have to give that some thought.

I returned to the bedroom, where I put on a new pair of lounging pajamas Mother had brought me, then reluctantly lay on the bed, hating the boredom of my confinement but determined to do what the doctor had ordered.

I glanced through the paper a second time before picking up the biography Janelle had loaned me: *A Man Called Peter*. She'd promised I would enjoy it far more than *Peyton Place*, the new novel everyone was talking about.

She was right. The book was absorbing, and I read quite a while before sleep overtook me.

I was awakened by a noise from outside. I sat up. No more noise but now I heard Gideon's angry voice, telling Heidi to get away. I brushed the open book off my chest and got out of bed, forcing myself to move slowly and carefully.

"Gideon?" I called before reaching the open front door.

"I'm okay," he replied in a terse tone.

I looked through the screen. Gideon sat on the ground, an overturned wheelbarrow beside him. Dirt and a large shrub had spilled out of the wheelbarrow and onto his lap. Heidi lay nearby, her muzzle flat on the ground between her paws, the expression in her eyes both guilty and remorseful.

I had to stifle a laugh. "What are you two doing?" I leaned a shoulder against the doorjamb.

Gideon looked around, as if not certain where my voice had come from, but finally, he found me. "I told Mrs. Andrus I'd move the shrubs from over there—" he jabbed his finger toward the fence— "to a shadier spot—" he pointed to the corner of the main house. "I hope she likes it when I'm done." He muttered something unintelligible beneath his breath as he held up both arms, revealing dozens of tiny scratches. "Man, that hurts."

"You need some salve on those."

"Yeah. These bushes are prickly. I should've worn a

long-sleeved shirt, but it's too hot." He started to get up, then fell over again.

I felt a twinge of alarm. "Gideon, are you hurt?" I pushed the screen door open a few inches in order to get a better look at him.

"No. I'm all right. Just hot, tired, and sweaty. And you need to get back to bed. You're supposed to stay off your feet, remember?"

"But you—"

"Go back to bed, Deb," he snapped. "I'm okay, and if the dog'll stay out of my way, I'll be able to finish the job. Take Heidi inside, will you?"

It was on the tip of my tongue to tell him he didn't need to get surly with me. I was merely concerned for his well-being. That's all. But somehow I managed to swallow the retort. Besides, who was working like a slave in the heat of the day and who was lying around like a princess?

I pushed the screen all the way open. "Come here, Heidi. Come on, girl."

Ears still flat, Heidi got up and slunk toward the house, slipping past me, a dog with the weight of the world on her back.

I told Heidi to lie down near the sofa; then I returned to my room, sat on the bed with pillows at my back, and pondered what I was going to do with my time while waiting for the baby to be born.

I couldn't lie around, day in and day out, reading books and twiddling my thumbs. I would go insane if I did. A few more days, and I would be allowed moderate activity. There had to be something constructive I could do with my time.

But what? My first priority was to the baby, not my own

willfulness. I would have to weigh all decisions against that measuring stick.

Maybe I needed to discern what God wanted me to learn from this experience. Patience, undoubtedly. Kindness and a gentleness of spirit, without question. An ability to be still and listen to His voice, most assuredly.

I sighed. "You have a great deal of work to do in me, Jesus. I wonder if I'm a hopeless case."

The telephone jangled and I answered it.

"Deborah?"

"Hello, Mother."

"Why are you answering the phone, dear? You should be in bed."

"I *am* in bed. Gideon installed a longer telephone cord last night so I can keep the telephone on the nightstand beside me." I could almost read my mother's thoughts—*Where is Gideon? Why isn't he there to answer the phone?*—so I answered before she could ask. "Gideon's working in the yard, and I've spent the morning reading."

"I should have come over today. You probably haven't eaten a thing."

Patience. Kindness and a gentle spirit. Listening for God's voice. "Gideon served me breakfast in bed. I promise you, I'm not starving. I'll let you know if I need anything. Honest."

"Well . . . all right. If you're sure."

A smile tweaked the corners of my mouth. "I'm sure."

"I don't suppose you'll be able to see the fireworks from your place."

"I doubt it. Too many trees." *We can take the baby to see them next year.* My heart fluttered with joy at the thought. "How about you and Dad? Are you going to the fairgrounds?"

"You know your father. He looks forward to the Fourth every year. He wouldn't miss the festivities for anything. Even the threat of thunderstorms doesn't stop him."

Some of my favorite childhood memories were of the Fourth of July, of riding on my dad's shoulders while watching the parade as it snaked through downtown on a hot afternoon, of licking an ice-cream cone while staring up at the colorful explosions in the sky after night fell.

Mother's voice drew me from my memories. "I'd better go, dear. My fried chicken needs turning. I'll see you in the morning."

"Okay. Give Dad my love."

As I hung up the phone, my stomach growled, and I thought, *Fried chicken does sound good.*

I heard the creak of the screen door, then Gideon's soft, "Hey, trouble," to Heidi. Moments later, he appeared in the bedroom doorway. His face, beaded with sweat, was red and blotchy. The raised scratches on his arms looked angry. "I'm gonna take a shower first. Then I'll fix something to eat. You hungry?"

"Famished."

"Won't take me long." He disappeared into the bathroom, closing the door behind him.

"The salve for your arms is in the medicine cabinet," I called.

My only answer was the sound of water spraying the sides of the shower stall.

I lay back, trying to ignore my stomach as it growled more insistently. Three more days of bed rest. Three more days and I could get up to fix myself something to eat whenever I was hungry. I wouldn't have to wait for someone else to do it for me. Besides, I felt guilty for making Gideon wait on me when he'd been working hard all morning. It felt wrong.

The next sounds that came from the bathroom were the unmistakable ones of someone—Gideon—falling in the shower. I got out of bed quickly, forgetting all instructions to the contrary, hurried across the room, and yanked open the bathroom door.

"Gideon!"

The shower curtain was parted enough that I could see he was on his back in the narrow stall, knees to chest, water pelting his head. His eyes were closed.

"Gideon, what happened?" I reached in and turned off the water. "Gideon?"

He opened his eyes, but his gaze didn't seem focused. Still, he managed to grin. "Man, I'm clumsy today. Maybe it wasn't Heidi's fault."

"Are you hurt?" I reached an arm toward him.

He motioned me off. "I'm okay. I just slipped. Must have been the soap."

"Can I help you up? Can I—"

"No lifting, remember?" He rubbed his face with his hands. "Besides, I'm okay. Bruised maybe, but okay."

I frowned as I stared at him. "Your eyes look . . . funny. Maybe you have a concussion."

His grin disappeared and his voice turned harsh. "Quit fussing over me, Deb. You're getting to be as bad as your mother."

That stung.

"Just close the door and let me get up on my own."

I beat a hasty retreat.

Norman Adams

I should've seen it coming, what happened. I should've read the signs.

One look at Gideon when he showed up for work that morning, and I should've told him to go straight home and get some sleep. I should've told him to tell the boss he was sick. I would've covered for him. Gideon's a good egg. All the guys on the crew like him.

But I didn't tell him to go home. I figured he'd stayed up late for the Fourth, doing a bit too much celebrating, same as me, and hadn't got himself enough sleep. Cup or two of coffee—the black stuff Charlene makes that's more fit to tar roads than to drink—and he'd wake up and be right as rain. That's what I figured.

It was a serious error in judgment on my part. No, that's being kind to myself. It was more than that. It was wrong what I did. Or rather, what I didn't do. I *chose* to ignore the signs, the truth, and choosing the way I did could've cost somebody their life. Could've cost Gideon his life.

Bad enough as it was, what happened.

CHAPTER TWENTY-SEVEN

Mother answered the phone when it rang that Thursday morning. She was in the living room. I was in the bedroom.

I heard her say, "Hello." A pause. "She can't come to the phone right now. This is her mother. May I help you?" Another pause. Then her voice dropped, and I couldn't hear what she was saying.

I didn't have to hear. When she appeared in my bedroom doorway a short while later, her face was ashen.

A horrid sense of *déjà vu* swept through me, chilling me to the bone. "Something's happened to Gideon."

"There's been an accident at the job site." Mother motioned with her hand, as if to make her words more clear. "The man who called said they've taken Gideon to the hospital."

"Mother, is he—" I couldn't finish. I couldn't say the words aloud.

"I was told it isn't too serious. Gideon's arm is broken, and he has some cuts and . . . oh, what was the word? I don't know. Anyway he should be all right after the doctor sees to him."

"Thank God," I whispered. "Oh, thank God." I got out of bed and reached for my capri pants and summer top.

"What do you think you're doing?"

"I'm going to the hospital, and you're going to drive me there."

I'm sure Mother wanted to argue, to refuse, but even she knew I needed to be with my husband.

"I'll get my pocketbook," she said, albeit with reluctance. "Move slowly, dear. We aren't in a race."

But we were, my heart told me. We were in a race, only not one I understood as yet.

God, don't let them be lying to me. Please keep Gideon safe. Don't take him from me.

The baby. Gideon.

Too much, God. It's too much.

Mother held my arm as she escorted me to her automobile. "The man who called asked for your doctor's name. I'm sure Dr. Ogilvie is already at the hospital by this time. You mustn't worry, Deborah. Worry isn't good for you or the baby."

That was the same advice Dr. Ogilvie had given me three days before.

So don't worry about tomorrow, the Bible said, *for tomorrow will bring its own worries. Today's trouble is enough for today.*

"Today's trouble is more than enough," I whispered. "Way more."

"What did you say, dear?"

"Nothing, Mother. Just hurry. Please hurry."

On Monday, I'd told the Lord I wanted to be a woman

of strong faith, and yet here I was, worried again. Fear was the opposite of faith, and yet I was drowning in it.

Please, God. Help me.

Mother drove to the hospital with deliberate care, never going even one mile per hour over the posted speed limit. I felt like screaming as I gripped the armrest on the passenger door. *Hurry. Hurry. Hurry.*

At last, we arrived. Despite Mother's best efforts to slow me down, I entered the ER with long, hurried strides. My own visit to this place had been barely over a week ago. I knew where to go.

At the desk, I told the fresh-faced receptionist my name, then, "They brought my husband here. There was an accident at work. Where—"

"Deborah."

I whirled around at the familiar—and comforting—sound of Dr. Ogilvie's voice. "Have you seen Gideon?" I demanded.

"Yes. I just left him."

"Where is he?"

"There's someone attending to him now. Why don't we step in here—" he motioned toward a small room off the public waiting area— "so we can talk privately."

A fresh wave of fear hit me.

Dr. Ogilvie glanced at Mother, who was by now standing near me. "I'd like to speak to your daughter alone, Mrs. Richardson." He gently grasped my elbow and steered me into the indicated room, closing the door behind us.

"It's more than a broken arm, isn't it?" My heart was in my throat. "Is he dying?"

Not like Andy. O God, not like Andy.

"Sit down, Deborah."

Please, God . . .

We sat side by side on the small beige sofa. On the wall opposite us—a wall the same color as the sofa—was a painting of Jesus in a house crowded with people. Men were lowering a crippled friend on a cot down through an opening in the roof so Jesus could heal him.

O God, please . . .

"Gideon is not dying, Deborah." The doctor took hold of my hand. "His injuries are surprisingly mild, considering the height from which he fell. I'm told it was at least twenty feet and probably more. He broke his left arm in three places, and he suffered some nasty cuts and contusions. But his injuries aren't life threatening."

My racing pulse began to slow.

Dr. Ogilvie frowned, his thick, nearly white eyebrows closing the space between them. "Deborah, your husband's accident was the result of his . . . of his intoxication."

"Intoxication?" I repeated the word as if it were from a foreign language.

"Yes."

"But . . . but that's impossible."

The doctor shook his head slowly. "I'm afraid not, Deborah. I believe he has a serious drinking problem."

"That's impossible. Gideon doesn't drink."

This time Dr. Ogilvie made no reply. He simply watched me with grave eyes.

A drinking problem? Impossible.

I remembered the evening of our wedding. He'd had some champagne, but when he knew it bothered me, he'd pushed it away. A person with a drinking problem wouldn't do that.

Intoxicated? Absurd.

I remembered the night of our first fight. He'd gone drinking with his friends, but he hadn't done that again. And even that night, he hadn't come home in a drunken stupor.

Drinking in the middle of the day? Not Gideon.

I remembered how he'd looked on the floor of the shower stall yesterday, crumpled like an accordion. Something about his eyes had been so strange.

O God . . . My prayer rose up again.

"Deborah, we can't help him if he doesn't see he has a problem."

But he doesn't have a problem, I wanted to protest. Besides, I couldn't be that stupid. I would have *known* if he had a drinking problem. Gideon had a job. He was a hard worker. He was intelligent and caring. Drunks were . . . drunks were bums, like the unkempt men one saw outside rescue missions. Gideon wasn't like them.

Another memory drifted into my thoughts, the memory of something Jack Clermont said the night he'd stayed with us: *"I was kind of worried about him after he got out of the army. . . . He was drinking too much."* I remembered the chill I'd felt at those words; I felt it again now.

Dr. Ogilvie cleared his throat as he released my hand. "I'll take you to see him."

I rose from the sofa, feeling stiff, so stiff that should anyone touch me I might shatter into a thousand pieces.

The doctor opened the door. Beyond it, I saw my mother, seated in a chair in the waiting area. Dad was with her. She must have called him. And there was Norm Adams off to the right of my parents. Norm must have come with Gideon to the hospital.

Those thoughts—and those people—seemed distant to me.

Like wisps of clouds one thinks could be touched but are in actuality far away.

I followed Dr. Ogilvie out of that small room, past the waiting area, and through a pair of wide doors. I was aware of the busyness of people all around me—nurses and doctors and orderlies. I knew we passed exam rooms and curtained areas where patients were hidden from my view. Yet I felt as if it were happening to someone else. Not me. Not to me.

And then I was with Gideon, standing at his bedside, seeing the stitches on his forehead, seeing the scrape on his right cheek, already bruising at the edges, seeing the cast that encompassed his left arm from biceps to wrist.

But I couldn't see his eyes because he didn't look at me. Wouldn't look at me.

"Stupid, huh?" he mumbled.

"What happened, Gideon?"

"Just a dumb accident. I wasn't paying attention to where I put the ladder. It wasn't on a firm foundation. When I leaned to get something, the whole thing toppled."

"Someone said you fell twenty feet."

He nodded, still not looking up. "Right over the side. I was lucky I didn't hit the pallet of bricks."

"Gideon?" I steeled myself, not wanting to ask but doing it anyway. "The doctor said . . . he said you'd been drinking. Is that true?"

He didn't answer me, not to confirm or to deny. He just covered his eyes with his right hand and didn't say a word.

This couldn't be happening. It couldn't be true. Gideon wouldn't do this. No one drank at this hour of the day. It had to be some horrible mistake. It couldn't be true. It couldn't be.

Gruffly, Gideon said, "Find out how soon we can go home, Deb. I want out of here."

My heart sank.

O God, save us!

Henry Richardson

One look at my daughter's face that day at the hospital while she was waiting for Gideon to be discharged and I could have gladly killed my son-in-law with my bare hands.

I didn't learn the facts about his accident from Deborah herself. Those I got from that fellow Gideon works with. Norm Adams, that's his name. Norm said he drove Gideon to the hospital, and he knew exactly what happened because he was there. He saw it all.

I took Norm over to a corner of that waiting room, away from my wife and everybody else, and I made him tell me everything. I think in my gut I already knew. When I heard Gideon was drinking on the job, I was fit to be tied. I don't know if I've ever felt such anger as I did at that moment.

Deborah had experienced more than her fair share of heartache. That was what Bernice said, and I agree. Our daughter didn't deserve this, too. And there she was, still in danger of miscarrying and supposed to be in bed, while Gideon was getting stinking drunk and trying to kill himself at work.

Too bad he failed. That was what I thought that day. Too bad he failed.

CHAPTER TWENTY-EIGHT

The silence in my mother's car was palpable.

Gideon reclined in the rear seat while I sat in the front, clutching the armrest on the passenger door as I had on the way to the hospital, though now for a different reason. Mother kept a death grip on the steering wheel throughout the drive home. She must have sensed that asking any questions would be futile.

She didn't like it one bit when I told her to go home after dropping us at our place. "At least let me come in and prepare your supper for later. You shouldn't—"

"No, Mother," I answered softly, watching Gideon as he walked toward the gate. "Gideon and I need to be alone so we can talk."

"Deborah, I—"

"Don't say anything, Mother. Please. Just don't say anything."

She sighed.

I got out of the car. "I'll call you in the morning. Don't come over until I call you."

"Deborah—"

"I'll call in the morning."

I pushed the car door closed and followed Gideon inside. He was lying on the couch, his right arm curved over his eyes, his right foot still touching the floor.

"You need to go to bed," he said.

"Gideon, we—"

He cut me off in the same manner I'd cut Mother off moments before. "Not now, Deb. My arm's throbbing, I hurt all over, and you shouldn't have been on your feet all this time. You shouldn't have come to the hospital." At last he moved his arm from his face. "Go lie down, Deb, and we'll sort through this later."

I nodded, too willing to flee rather than face a danger I could not comprehend.

In the bedroom, I kicked off my sandals, then shed my pants and cotton top and crawled beneath the top sheet. I rolled onto my side, clutching my pillow to my chest, and buried my face in the downy softness.

It'll be all right. We'll straighten everything out when he isn't in pain. We'll talk and we'll sort through the misunderstanding and it'll be all right.

Did I believe what I was telling myself? Certainly I *wanted* to believe it.

O God, please help us.

———

I fell asleep in my misery, and the next thing I remember was hearing the deep rumble of men's voices, softly spoken, coming from the other room. Feeling disoriented, I sat up. The heat in the bedroom was stifling; I'd forgotten to turn on the fan before getting into bed.

"You could've killed yourself, Gideon."

"Well, I didn't."

"Worse, you could've killed somebody else. Did you think of that?"

"I'm the one who got hurt."

"You and Mac."

Gideon's voice altered slightly. "Mac?"

"Yeah, Mac. He got smacked in the head with the ladder when you went flying off it the other direction. Lucky for you it wasn't anything serious."

"I didn't know."

"You didn't know anything, man. You were too blasted."

"I *wasn't* blasted."

I got out of bed, slipped into my clothes, and walked across the room. The door was cracked several inches, and I could see Norm Adams through the opening. He stood with his legs braced apart and his arms crossed over his chest. His angry glare never wavered as he stared in the direction of the couch. I stopped in my tracks, not certain whether or not I should make my presence known.

"Do you believe what you're saying?" Norm demanded.

I'd never heard Gideon swear before, but he did so now. I covered my mouth as if I'd been the one to speak the foul word. The motion gave me away. Norm's head turned toward me, and our gazes met.

I opened the door the rest of the way and walked into the living room.

When Gideon saw me, he said, "You're supposed to be lying down. Bed rest, remember?"

I ignored him. "Hello, Norm."

"I drove Gideon's truck over. It was still at the job site." Norm jerked his head toward the street. "His tools and things are in the back."

"You said someone else was hurt?"

"Yeah, but not too serious. I heard he's got a lump on his head the size of a golf ball." Norm's gaze was sympathetic. "Sorry about this, on top of your worries about the baby and all."

Funny, in a way, that he was apologizing for something he had no part in. Why do people do that?

"Oh, I almost forgot." Norm reached into his shirt pocket. "Here's Gideon's final paycheck." He held it toward me, and I took it. "They paid him through today even though he only worked a couple of hours." He looked at Gideon. "The boss didn't have to do that, you know? You're lucky he didn't have you arrested."

I turned toward Gideon, feeling sick to my stomach. "You lost your job?"

"I'll get another one." He stood, his expression an odd cross between belligerence and uncertainty.

Norm said, "I'll be going now. One of the guys is waiting outside to drive me home."

I'm not sure if I acknowledged his comment. My mind was in a whirl, my stomach churning.

What were we supposed to do now that both of us were unemployed? How were we to pay for the hospital and doctor expenses we'd incurred in the past eight days? What were we to do about rent and groceries and utilities and gas for the truck?

I found myself sitting on the couch, my legs too shaky to

support me a moment longer. Norm had left quickly and quietly, and I was alone with Gideon.

He went to the kitchen sink, filled a glass with water, and drank it in one long series of gulps. He refilled it before turning to face me. He leaned his backside against the counter, took a few more sips from the water glass, then adjusted his broken arm in the sling, wincing in pain as he did so.

What's happening to us?

"We'll be okay, Deb."

"How?"

"I don't know, but we will."

I unfolded his paycheck and stared at the amount. "The rent's due. This won't cover it."

"I'll get another job. This one wasn't so great anyway."

You always liked your job.

After a long silence, he said, "We could sell the farm. That would cover things for quite a while."

"The farm," I whispered, remembering my daydream of a few days ago, the daydream of a toddler tottering through the grass beside the farmhouse. I sat up a little straighter. "No, we won't sell it." I looked at Gideon. "We'll move back there to live."

"What?"

"We'll move back there right away. We wouldn't have any rent to pay, and once you're able to work, you can find something in Amethyst or on one of the other farms in the area. There's always someone in need of a carpenter or a handyman." I pictured the farm at sunrise, heard the buzzing and chirruping of insects and the twittering of birds in the trees. "Next spring, I can plant a garden to help feed us. And chickens. We'll replace the chickens."

"Wait a minute, Deb. That's crazy. I'm no—"

"It isn't crazy. It must be why I've resisted selling it all along. God was looking out for us. He was making sure we'd have a place to go when . . . when all of . . . of *this* . . . happened."

Gideon set his glass on the counter. "You're getting way ahead of yourself."

"I'm not getting ahead of myself." I stood. "If we sell the farm, soon enough we'll have nothing." Fear of the unknown future hit me like a sledge. "But if we live there, we'll always have our home." *We'll be safe there,* I silently added.

Gideon turned and looked out the window above the sink.

"Remember last summer? Remember how you came to the farm and made all those repairs that were needed so badly?" There was an anxious whine in my voice. "You liked it, Gideon. You were happy doing that work. Remember?"

Had he liked it? Or had he only done it to impress me, to win my affection?

I shoved away my doubts and pressed on. "I want to go home to the farm, Gideon. I want to go ho—" The rest of the sentence caught in my throat, choked on the sob I hadn't known was there.

"Let's sleep on it tonight, Deb. If it's still how you feel in the morning, then . . . then we'll talk about it some more."

Janelle Burns

I learned about Gideon's accident—and the cause of it—in a roundabout fashion. It came to me through a friend of a friend. That was when I understood why I'd taken an instant liking to Gideon Clermont. He reminded me of my brother

Willie. My alcoholic brother. Willie can charm a person's socks off too.

O God, I prayed when that realization hit me. *Be merciful!*

I tried to get Deborah to open up, to talk about what had happened and what was still happening, but she refused. She let Gideon lie to her, and then she lied to herself.

Denial is a tool of the devil, who is a liar and the father of lies. He hates the truth, and he hates those who belong to Jesus. I knew he was prowling around Deborah and Gideon, seeking to devour them.

I'd circled that block of denial with Willie enough times to know how futile any attempt on my part to help matters would be until Deborah was good and ready to listen.

So I did what I could. I let her know I was her friend, same as I'd done when I was encouraging her to return to fellowship with the Lord and with other believers. I let her know in every way I could think of that I loved her and would be there for her whenever she needed me. I offered her a shoulder to cry on and a sympathetic ear to listen if she wanted to talk.

Ted and I helped the Clermonts move to the farm that July. I know her folks loaned them money to help them "through the rough patch." I prayed to God it would be the only time they needed to borrow money. I prayed to God Gideon would get better rather than worse. I thought of my baby brother, serving time in prison because of what he'd done in an alcoholic rage, and I prayed to God Deborah wouldn't ever have to visit her husband behind steel bars.

CHAPTER TWENTY-NINE

It was going to be okay.

We were going to be okay.

Oh, things were awkward—strained—between Gideon and me in those first weeks after we moved back to the farm. He was restless and impatient. I was worried and fretful. Neither of us wanted to talk about what happened, about his accident and why he'd lost his job. So we said nothing at all.

Little by little, things settled into a routine of sorts. It took a while, but Gideon eventually accepted that the farm was our home for the time being. I knew that he'd come to that point when he said he planned to remodel the second bedroom upstairs into a nursery once the cast was off his arm.

In early September, Gideon was hired to help build a new house in town for Knute Peterman and his large family. The work would last into early winter.

We were going to be okay.

I pulled my oversized sweater over my rounded belly as I lowered myself onto the top step of the back porch. Supper waited on the stove, but Gideon hadn't returned from work yet. I took a deep breath, staring toward the sun as it settled lower in the western sky. The dusty haze of harvesttime glowed gold-orange above the cooling earth.

Tomorrow, my parents were coming for a visit. It was my dad's birthday, but this year, they were driving to the farm rather than Gideon and me going into Boise for Mom's usual birthday dinner.

"You don't need that long drive, Deborah," my mother had insisted. "Next year, you can bring the baby to the party. This year, we'll come to you."

I closed my eyes, letting my thoughts drift back one year, to the night Gideon was my escort to Dad's party, to the night of our first kiss, to the night he asked me to give us a chance.

So much had happened in the past year. So much.

O God, I love Gideon, and I want to be a good wife to him. Reveal to me what that means.

Beside me, Heidi sat up, then stood. By the time my eyes were open, she'd scampered down the steps, then stopped and was waiting for Gideon's truck to roll to a stop. I lifted a hand to wave at him.

"How was your day?" I called as he stepped out of the cab.

He strode toward me. "I've got a bad headache and my arm's killing me. I'm going to lie down."

"Dinner's ready. Don't you—"

"No. I'm not hungry right now. I'll eat later." He moved past me with barely a glance to spare.

I tried not to let my feelings be hurt, but I failed. I wanted him to take me in his arms as he had a year ago. I wanted him to kiss me with passion. I wanted him to tell me how glad he was that we were husband and wife and that we were having a baby. I wanted him to . . .

I smothered a sigh. The things I wanted were, no doubt, childish and sentimental.

I rose and followed Gideon into the house and up the stairs. He was lying on the bed, still fully clothed, an arm slung over his eyes.

"Is there anything I can get you?" I asked. "Perhaps an ice pack."

"No."

"All right." I turned toward the door. "I . . . I'll keep your dinner warm for you."

"Don't bother, Deb. Put it away. When I'm hungry, I can warm it up for myself."

As I descended the stairs, I remembered something else from one year before. I remembered Gideon, resting one foot on the bottom step of my porch, saying, *"You look very pretty tonight, Deborah Haskin."* I remembered the way I'd blushed, the way I'd thought how nice he looked, too, in his suit and tie, his dark hair slicked back. I remembered his outstretched hand as he said, *"Your white horse awaits."* I remembered my smile when I realized Gideon Clermont was a romantic at heart.

But where's the romance now?

The thought made me feel small, petty, selfish. Gideon didn't feel well, and I was angry at him for not playing the knight on a prancing steed.

In the kitchen, I took a plate from the cupboard and carried it to the stove. I cut myself a thin slice of ham and spooned peas and pearl onions onto the plate. Then I added a dollop of mashed potatoes topped with melting butter and carried my dinner to the table.

I wasn't hungry, and I barely touched my food, other than to push it from one side of my plate to the other with a fork. Why had I bothered to cook? No one was going to eat.

Gideon, what's happened to us? Why are things so . . . so different than they were before? Why are you *so different?*

Of course, maybe my husband wasn't different. Maybe I was the one who'd changed. Or maybe neither one of us was who we'd pretended to be. Maybe . . .

"Here, Heidi." I set my plate on the floor. "Enjoy."

While the dog licked the plate clean, I went to the stove, where I wrapped the rest of the uneaten dinner in foil and put it in the refrigerator. Then I washed the dishes, leaving them to air dry. Finally, I filled a bag with ice cubes and took it, along with the aspirin bottle and a glass of water, upstairs.

As I stepped into the bedroom doorway, I saw that Gideon was sitting on the side of the bed, his back toward me. Two more steps, and I saw a vodka bottle in his right hand as he poured the clear liquid into the glass in his left.

I must have gasped, although I wasn't aware of it. But something caused him to look over his shoulder.

There was a painful silence before I whispered, "Gideon?"

He looked surprised, then guilty, and finally, defiant as his eyes narrowed and the line of his mouth thinned. He turned away, lifting the glass to his lips and draining it before setting it on the nightstand. Then he screwed the top back on the liquor bottle. "I needed something to dull the pain in my head. It's not the end of the world, Deb. Having a drink isn't a mortal sin."

"Where . . . where did you get it?"

"Where do you think? I bought it."

I stepped farther into the room. "But you said . . . but after what happened—"

"Stop nagging me, Deb. I've had a long day, and I'm in pain. My head and my arm's killing me. Can't a man get a little relief without being harangued to death?"

This wasn't the first drink he'd had today. That knowledge, that certainty, sliced through me, nearly drowning me. I wanted to reject it, but I couldn't.

I said aloud what I'd been thinking earlier. "What's happened to us?"

"Nothing. It's just a drink." He dropped the liquor bottle into the drawer of the nightstand, then slammed it closed.

There were tears in my eyes, but the last thing I wanted to do was cry.

Gideon stood and looked at me again. His belligerent countenance softened. "Come on, Deb. You're making a mountain out of a molehill."

Am I?

"Look, I'm sorry. I wasn't trying to do anything underhanded." He motioned behind him, toward the nightstand and the hidden vodka bottle. "My pain pills are gone, and now that I'm working again, I need something for the pain. A drink does that for me." He moved to stand before me, placing his hands on my shoulders. "Even the Bible says a little wine is good for the stomach that ails you. If it can be for that purpose, why not for pain?"

My spirit told me he was twisting Scripture for his own purpose, but my heart longed to give him the benefit of the doubt.

Gideon brushed my forehead with his lips. "Let me rest a bit longer. I'll come downstairs after a while, and we can talk some more about this if you really feel the need. Okay?" He took the ice pack from my hand while kissing my forehead a second time. Then he turned me toward the bedroom door and gave me a gentle push.

I was halfway down the stairs before I realized that he'd manipulated me.

Why, I wondered, was I the one who felt guilty when he was the one in the wrong?

— *Clyde Beekman* —

Despite the circumstances that brought the Clermonts back to their farm, Vera and I were delighted to have them as part of our community again. But our delight dimmed when Gideon didn't attend Sunday services with Deborah.

At first she made excuses for him because of his accident, but after a time, when I asked how Gideon was doing, she would simply shrug her shoulders, give the slightest shake of her head, and say nothing.

I decided to pay a call to the Clermont farm one Sunday afternoon. I thought extending a hand of friendship toward Gideon might help.

CHAPTER THIRTY

Gideon had left a note for me on the kitchen table:

> Went fishing. With any luck, plan on trout for supper. Back
> no later than 3:00. G.

He could go fishing but he couldn't go to church. And he
knew my parents were coming at five o'clock for Dad's birthday
dinner. How could he be so thoughtless? How could he go fishing today of all days? I'd tried to be understanding about his
refusal to go to church with me, but now I was furious.

I was still fuming two hours later when he came in the back
door, holding a string of fish, proudly displayed. But it was the
slightly off-kilter look in his eyes that caught my attention and
caused every nerve ending in my body to screech.

"Behold, I come bearing food." He set his tackle box on the
floor next to the door, then carried the fish to the sink.

Wordlessly, I stared at his back as he turned on the cold water and began to clean the fish. I don't think he noticed my silence. *Don't let it be true. God, don't let it be true.*

Was it the Lord who drew me across the kitchen to that tackle box? I don't know. I only know that I went, squatted beside it, and opened the lid. There were two vodka bottles in the bottom, under a spare reel and a pair of gloves. One was empty. One was almost full. I took hold of the latter with my left hand, stood, and faced the sink. My earlier anger remained, but it had turned cold, a cold so intense it stole all sensation from my body.

"Why, Gideon?"

"Why what?" He didn't look at me. Just kept washing those slimy, bug-eyed, smelly fish.

I twisted the cap with my right hand and removed it from the bottle. "Why would you do it?"

"Sorry. Can't hear you over the water."

Stiffly, I walked to the sink, stopping beside him. As I turned the vodka bottle bottom-side up and dumped the contents over the fish, I shouted, *"Why?"* in his ear.

He jumped back, startled. His hands dripped water onto the floor. "What are you—" He stopped, then reached for the bottle, as if wanting to save the precious liquid before it could all go down the drain.

Rather than let him have it, I slammed it into the sink, shattering the glass.

"Deb!"

"Don't you 'Deb' me. Don't you try to talk your way out of this. Don't you blame it on a pain in your arm or a headache or anything else. Gideon, look at what you're doing. This is what cost you your job. This is what caused your accident."

A shadow covered his face. "No, it isn't."

I took a step backward. "Do you honestly believe what you're saying? Don't you understand what you're doing to yourself? Don't you care what you're doing to *us?*"

"You're the one who doesn't understand. The way you nag would drive any man to drink."

He may as well have struck me. The pain was the same. If I'd still been holding the bottle, I would have thrown it at him instead of into the sink.

Gideon picked up a dish towel and dried his hands, then shut off the running water, plunging the kitchen into silence. "Look, I'm sorry. I didn't mean that."

Didn't you?

"I just don't see why you're making a big deal out of an occasional drink."

Occasional?

"I can stop any time I want to, you know. I don't *have* to drink."

"Then don't."

His scowl returned.

"Stop, Gideon. On our wedding day you told me you wouldn't drink champagne if it bothered me. Do you remember that? Well, it bothers me. Don't do it."

It was at that moment we both heard the car coming up our driveway.

O God, don't let it be my parents. It's too early. Don't let them come early.

Holding my breath, one hand pressed against my collarbone, I walked to the back door and looked outside.

"It's Pastor Clyde," I said, my voice breaking, not sure if his arrival was better than if it were my parents . . . or worse.

"Oh, great. Just what I need. Somebody else to preach at me."

Clyde Beekman would take one look at Gideon and know what was going on. He would know my husband was tipsy in the middle of a Sunday afternoon.

I couldn't bear the shame of it.

I whirled toward Gideon. "Go upstairs. I'll make your excuses."

"Wha—"

"Go on. Hurry, before he sees you."

"I'm not running off like a dog with its tail tucked between its legs. This is *my* home, too. I've got a right to stay in my own kitchen when I feel like it."

"Gideon, please."

He didn't budge. Not an inch. There was no give in him, no consideration, no tenderness.

"Hello," Pastor Clyde called from beyond the porch.

Dreading the moment, I turned, hoping my smile didn't look as forced as it felt. "How nice to see you, Pastor." I pushed open the screen. "Come on in, won't you?"

"Hope you don't mind me dropping by this way."

"Not at all." Ordinarily, that would have been the truth.

Pastor Clyde entered the house. "Gideon, glad to see you." He stepped toward my husband. "How's your arm?" He held out his hand to shake Gideon's.

"It's all right." Gideon didn't take the pastor's hand. "Sorry. I'm a bit fishy." He jerked his head toward the sink.

I wondered if Clyde Beekman could see the shattered vodka bottle. I wondered if he could smell the liquor over the stink of fish. I wondered if he could tell that Gideon's eyes were glassy.

"Ah." Pastor Clyde lowered his arm. "You're working on the Peterman house, I hear."

Gideon nodded.

"Well, that's good news." He turned toward me. "I didn't have a chance after service to ask how you're doing, Deborah."

"I'm well, thank you, Pastor." I placed a hand on my abdomen. "The baby's getting more active. The doctor is guardedly confident I'll be able to carry to term now."

"'Children born to a young man are like sharp arrows in a warrior's hands. How happy is the man whose quiver is full of them!' Psalm 127."

Gideon laughed. "In this little house, the quiver'll be full with just one kid."

Something flickered across Pastor Clyde's face.

He knows.

I wished the floor would open up and swallow me whole.

Bernice Richardson

I'm telling you, I was terribly upset when my daughter cancelled dinner for her father's birthday. Not that I wanted to add any pressure to her life. It's just that my instincts told me she wasn't speaking the whole truth.

"Gideon has the flu, Mother. He's throwing up. I don't want you and Dad exposed."

"What about you, dear? You can't afford to get sick at this stage of your pregnancy."

There was a lengthy silence on the other end of the line before she answered, "Don't worry. I won't catch it." Then she hurriedly said good-bye and hung up.

CHAPTER THIRTY-ONE

Gideon didn't actually pour his drinks in front of me after the day Pastor Clyde came to call, but he didn't go to great pains to hide what he was doing, either. By his actions, he silently said, *If I choose to drink, I will. Leave me alone, woman.*

Maybe he was right. Maybe I was overreacting. But I didn't think so, and I let him know I didn't think so. Alcohol changed him, made him irritable. Or maybe it was my harping that made him irritable. At least that's what he told me, over and over and over again.

Our home became an armed camp, and Gideon and I became snipers, ready to fire a verbal round at each other without warning. And fire we did. We wounded with words. We became experts at it, learning the other's vulnerable spots, and then taking advantage of the knowledge.

I hated the way we were living.

I hated the things I thought.
I hated the words I spoke.
I hated the way I felt.
I hated . . .
No, I wouldn't let myself go that far.
Not then. Not yet.

On a Saturday in late October, the ladies of Amethyst Community Church held a baby shower in my honor. Gideon brought me to town and dropped me off at the church, promising to return for me at four o'clock.

I stood on the sidewalk and watched as he drove away, not moving until the truck turned the corner and disappeared from view. It was almost a relief to see him go, almost a relief to not have to wonder, for the next few hours, when we would launch into another quarrel.

With a discouraged sigh, I turned and climbed the steps to the front door of the church.

Inside, I followed the sounds of women's voices to the fellowship hall. Pausing, I looked around the room. About a dozen women were there, including my mother and Janelle Burns, gathered in small groups or busily attending to last-minute preparations. The hall had been decorated with pink and blue streamers from one end to the other, and helium-filled balloons bobbed at the corners of a long table covered with pretty packages of varying sizes. The festive mood was contagious, and to my surprise, my spirits lifted.

"Here she is!" Vera Beekman exclaimed when she saw me.

The volume of conversations in the room increased as I was greeted and hugged and escorted to a place of honor.

It wasn't long before Alice Gordon had us playing a very silly game. By the end, my dress was covered from collar to hemline with clothespins and all of the women were laughing so hard they had tears in their eyes.

"Now the gifts," Vera announced after snapping a picture of me with her Brownie camera. "Susan, will you record them for Deborah?"

Susan Sutherland, the wife of one of the church elders, agreed and sat down next to me, paper and pen in hand. For the next thirty minutes, she was kept quite busy, too, as I removed ribbons and bows and carefully lifted tape from the wrapping paper to reveal what was inside. There was a hand-made crocheted baby blanket from Alice. A white bassinet and two dozen diapers from my mother. A beautiful framed print of a smiling Jesus surrounded by little children from Janelle. A pale yellow layette—tiny hat and little booties and soft body shirt—from Martha Kern. Handmade building blocks from Patty Thompson. Rattles and toys and bibs and receiving blankets and bottles and more.

Their generosity and thoughtfulness overwhelmed me. I felt loved and cherished for a change, a feeling I wanted to last.

But, of course, the shower eventually had to end. The women hugged me and kissed my cheeks and returned to their own homes and families. Mother and Janelle, who had come to Amethyst together, offered to drive me to the farm, but I declined, telling them Gideon was coming for me soon and we would need the truck in order to carry all of my wonderful gifts home.

Only Gideon didn't come at four o'clock as he'd promised. Nor was he there by four-thirty. At five, Vera Beekman insisted on taking me home.

I sat in the front seat of her automobile with my hands clenched and my gaze turned out the passenger window.

"Deborah," Vera said softly, "if you need to talk, I'm a good listener."

I shook my head. After all, what could I tell her? That his failure to come for me was just one more in a string of thoughtless acts? That Gideon and I couldn't seem to do anything but fight? If I admitted that, I would have to admit why we fought. I couldn't do that. I was so . . . so ashamed. If I were a better person, if I were more submissive, if I didn't lose my temper so easily, if I were a better wife, surely things wouldn't be so bad, surely Gideon wouldn't feel the need to—

"You're sure you don't want to talk?"

"Yes," I managed to answer. "Everything is fine. Gideon just got busy and lost track of time." It was a feeble excuse, but it was the best I could do.

When Vera pulled up to our house a short while later, there was no sign of Gideon, though the truck was parked near the barn, so I knew he was at home. Heidi, who'd been lying by the back door, came off the porch and trotted over to the car, welcoming me with a wag of her tail.

"Would you like to call Gideon to take your gifts into the house?" Vera asked.

With her words a horrid sense of dread twisted my stomach. "No. We can manage on our own. Let's just put everything on the porch. Gideon can bring it inside when he's . . . when he's not busy."

"But I don't mind taking—"

"Really, Vera. I insist. We'll set everything on the porch for now."

I suppose she heard the anxiety in my voice for she didn't

argue after that. In silence, we took the bounty of gifts from the trunk and carried them to the back porch, leaving them in a pile near the top step.

When we were done, Vera gave me a hug as she said good-bye. She couldn't hide the concern in her eyes, but she kept her thoughts to herself. I remained outside until she was back on the road heading for town. Then with a heavy heart, I went inside.

Gideon was in the living room, asleep on the floor near the sofa.

No, not asleep.

Passed out. I saw the glass, tipped onto its side, the last dregs of its contents staining the rug.

"Gideon, how could you?"

He didn't stir.

I walked over to him and gave his shoulder a small shove with the toe of my shoe. "Gideon."

Still no response.

This time, I nudged him harder. "Gideon!"

He groaned, and his eyes fluttered but didn't open.

I struck his upper arm with my handbag. "How could you? How could you do this to me?"

He didn't budge, hadn't felt a thing.

I swung my purse harder this time, striking his arm again.

He didn't even know I was there. He was out, stone cold.

I wanted to kick him. But if I did, I was afraid I wouldn't ever be able to stop.

Sobbing now, I raced up the stairs as fast as my legs would carry me. There, I dropped onto the bed and buried my face in the pillow.

I hope he lies there and rots.

I had known grief when Andy died, but this was different.

This was grief mixed with rage and despair and guilt and shame. Andy hadn't chosen to hurt me by dying, but Gideon was choosing. He chose to hurt me every time he took a drink.

What was I to do? Nothing. There was nothing I could do. I felt trapped. Trapped in a marriage unraveling at the seams. I was pregnant and unable to work and my husband was a . . . a . . .

O God, help me! What am I to do now?

I cried myself to sleep.

———

Dawn was creeping into the bedroom when Gideon appeared in the doorway. As if my body had been awaiting this moment, I came instantly awake. I sat up, staring at him, heartsick, exhausted.

"How'd you get home yesterday?" he asked.

"Vera brought me."

"Did she . . . " He let the question drift off, unfinished.

"She didn't see you. I wouldn't let her come in."

He raked the fingers of his right hand through his hair. "I'm sorry."

"You're sorry," I echoed softly.

"Look, I . . . " He took one step into the bedroom. "Deb, I love you."

The words were meaningless to me. He must have seen that in my eyes.

"I never meant for this to get out of hand the way it has. I . . . I don't know what got into me."

"Vodka got into you." The words dripped with sarcasm.

Gideon drew a deep breath. As he let it out, he said, "Yeah. I know."

Now was when I should have struck him with my purse.
Now, when he was conscious. Now, when he could feel it.
Now, when he could see how hurt I was.

"I'm gonna stop, Deb. I'm through. I promise."

I moved to the side of the bed, not wanting to look at him.

"I'll never take another drink."

Tears welled in my eyes, and my throat constricted.

Gideon entered the room. When he reached my side of the
bed, he knelt on the floor before me, then took hold of my right
hand between both of his. Reluctantly, I met his gaze.

"Deb, I'm sorry. You're everything to me. I love you more
than I thought it was possible to love anyone. I don't know why
I've fought you so hard about . . . about the drinking. It isn't
even that important to me. I'm not going to fight you anymore.
I'm going to straighten up. I won't ever take another drink.
I'll start going to church with you, too. I know I need to.
I'm going to be the best husband any woman ever had and the
best dad any kid ever had. I promise you, Deb." He searched
my eyes; then he added softly, "I'm sorry. More sorry than I
can say. Can you forgive me?"

What else could I do? He was my husband. He was the
father of our unborn child. I loved him, despite everything.
Of course I would forgive him.

And I wanted, so very desperately, to believe him.

PART THREE

1957

Without wavering, let us hold tightly

to the hope we say we have,

for God can be trusted to keep His promise.

HEBREWS 10:23

CHAPTER THIRTY-TWO

Our daughter, Sharon Rose Clermont, arrived two weeks ahead of schedule, at five in the morning, January 1, 1957, the first baby of the new year. The ride to the hospital in Boise was a harrowing one. The roads were covered with snow and ice, and more than once, I felt as if Gideon were about to lose control of the truck completely. But he was sober. He'd kept his promise to stop drinking.

—

Our son, Peter Alan Clermont, was born at seven at night on December 31, 1957, the last baby of the old year. The ride to the hospital was less frightening in the daylight, with clear roads. And Gideon still seemed in full control—of both the vehicle and of himself.

Thank You, Jesus.

PART FOUR

1961

I am losing all hope;

I am paralyzed with fear.

PSALM 143:4

CHAPTER THIRTY-THREE

"Sharon Rose," I called. "Take your brother's hand, right this instant. And don't either of you go near the street. Sharon Rose, are you listening to me?"

"I'll get them," Gideon offered. "Meet you at the car." Then he hurried down the steps.

I turned toward Pastor Clyde, hoping I didn't look as harried as I felt. "It was a wonderful Mother's Day service, Pastor. Thank you for the lovely carnations."

"You're most welcome, Deborah. I wish we could do more to honor the mothers in our congregation." His gaze moved toward Gideon and the children. "Your family looks well."

I heard the inevitable question within the comment: *How are things going at home? Is Gideon doing okay?*

"Yes," I said, putting on a smile. "Everyone's well." I stepped away. "I'd better go. Perhaps I'll see you Tuesday morning." Tuesdays at ten were when the women's group met in the church basement.

A gust of wind nearly swept my hat from my head as I walked toward the parking lot. I quickly placed my right hand on the crown. I wouldn't want this hat to get ruined. It was a favorite of mine. In fact, I thought it rather sad that hats seemed to be going out of fashion.

Gideon already had the children settled into the backseat of our Nash. Mother had given us the automobile when Dad bought her a new car three years before.

I thought how handsome Gideon looked in his gray suit and pale blue shirt. He was leaning against the car, one ankle crossed over the other, his arms folded across his chest. His black hair had been mussed by the breeze, giving him a roguish appearance. His face was already tanned from long hours spent in the sunshine. He looked . . . he looked good.

As I drew near, Gideon pulled open the driver's door. "Ready to go?"

"Yes. I'm ready. It was a wonderful service, didn't you think?"

Nearly every Sunday I asked the same question.

"Sure. Real nice." He slid behind the wheel and turned the key in the ignition.

Nearly every Sunday that was his same response.

I got into the car, suppressing a sigh. It was a glorious spring day, and I didn't want anything to spoil it. Last Mother's Day we'd had snow, hail, and rain within that twenty-four-hour period, and Gideon hadn't gone with us to church because he'd had the flu. Again.

But today was perfect. Not a cloud in the cerulean sky, a blue so bright it almost hurt my eyes. The breeze, gusty at times, felt pleasant mixed with the warmth of the sun.

Gideon drove through Amethyst, headed east. Past the bank and the Rialto Theater and Julia's Café. Past the mayor's new home and the arena where they held junior rodeos each summer. Past the new high school and the aging grade school. And finally into the irrigated farmlands that stretched for miles in all directions.

"Children, look." I pointed toward the pasture on my side of the road. "Mr. Thomas has another new colt. See it?"

"I don't see it, Mommy. Where?" Peter asked.

"Right there." I touched Gideon's arm with my left hand. "Honey, slow down so Peter has a chance to see."

Gideon made an impatient sound in his throat, but he complied.

"See, Peter?" I pointed again. "The little black-and-white colt. Right there. See him?"

"Ooooh," he squealed, as only a three-year-old can.

Joy rose in my chest. How I loved being a mother. How I loved being Sharon Rose's mother and Peter's mother. I'd wanted children before I became pregnant, but I hadn't known having them would make me feel so . . . so special, so unique, so complete.

Not that there hadn't been difficult times during the past five years. There had. Having two babies so close together, being a farmer's wife, taking care of the house, tending the garden and the animals, budgeting the accounts, paying the bills—sometimes it seemed more than overwhelming.

But on days like today, I was content.

For I have learned how to get along happily whether I have much or little. . . . For I can do everything with the help of Christ who gives me the strength I need.

What would I have done without the help of Christ in the past five years? I couldn't imagine. I didn't want to imagine.

I wouldn't have had the strength to go on without the help of my Lord.

A cloud passed over the glow of my contentment. Remembrances better left forgotten. Besides, Gideon was doing better now. Much better. Just as he'd promised.

Promised . . . again.

Two years ago, Gideon had taken over the planting and harvesting of crops on our land. He'd become a competent farmer, despite himself. He earned extra money with odd jobs and carpentry work around the area. He went to church with me and the children most Sundays, and occasionally he made it to one of the potluck suppers the church ladies held. Other times the children and I went without him.

Too often we go without him.

I cast a surreptitious glance at my husband.

Gideon loved me and the children. I knew that. He wanted good things for us. He wanted good things for himself. If only I could erase those moments of doubt. If only . . .

I suppressed a sigh.

We weren't the family we should be. Gideon and I didn't have the marriage either of us had hoped for. Or even the marriage we'd had at the beginning. There was a wall between us, a wall we'd constructed ourselves, brick by brick. Mine were bricks of fear and distrust, a kind of self-protection against another disappointment.

And there had been disappointments. Gideon had struggled to keep his promise to never take another drink. He'd failed a time or two, but he was always remorseful when I learned the truth. He always promised me again, and I would try to hope again. And surely he'd succeeded at last. Surely God had answered my prayers. Surely we would be okay.

We arrived at the farm, and Gideon pulled the old Nash into the detached garage he'd built three summers ago. Wordlessly, he got out of the car, then opened the rear door. The children slid off the seat, their short legs churning before they even hit the ground.

"Into the house, you two," I called. "You need to change your clothes."

Gideon fell into step beside me as we left the garage.

"Will it be a while before dinner?" he asked. "I've got some work to do in the barn."

Why don't you spend the afternoon with me and the children? Remember when you used to want to spend time with me? I pressed my lips together so I wouldn't speak the reprimand aloud.

O God, help me not to be a nagging wife. Help me to respect my husband, to build up rather than tear down. Help me to . . . to have faith.

"Deb, did you hear me?"

I looked at him. "I'm sorry, Gideon. I was . . . I was lost in thought."

"I asked if there was time for me to get some work done in the barn before dinner."

"It'll be about an hour." I saw Peter veer off the porch and head for the swing. "Peter!"

I shoved my pocketbook into Gideon's arms and headed after our son. I really didn't want grass stains on his best Sunday slacks again. I caught him in the nick of time.

"No you don't, young man," I said, squeezing him tight. "Not this time."

Thoughts that had turned grim during the drive back to the farm were forgotten in the pleasure of holding my son.

— *Gertrude Johnson* —

I've said before that I'm no gossip, and that's the honest truth. But mercy me, I must tell you, I did worry about my young neighbor. It seemed to me Deborah carried the burden of her family on her slim shoulders.

I couldn't quite figure out that husband of hers. Gideon was likable enough, but I couldn't say I'd gotten to know him well, even after being his neighbor these past five years. Pleasant one time you saw him, moody and disagreeable the next. That was Gideon Clermont.

Course, maybe he had a right to be moody and grumpy, sick as he was so often. I didn't know what ailed him, but I lost track of the times I heard Deborah say he couldn't be somewheres 'cause he was sick in bed. He always had aches and pains and ailments of one sort or another. Mighty sad for a young man like him. I did hope it wasn't anything serious.

Like I said already, Deborah carried the burden for her little family on her slim shoulders, and I worried about her.

CHAPTER THIRTY-FOUR

From the beginning of my Christian walk—with the exception of that dark period after Andy's death when I allowed my love for Jesus to grow cold—I've preferred to meet with the Lord early in the morning. This quiet hour became even more important after my children were born. Time alone was a precious commodity.

In the summer months, I often took my Bible outside, where I sat on the porch or strolled down to the shallow creek at the far end of our land. But this May morning, rain pelted the northwest side of the house with ferocity, and so I was glad to settle into my favorite chintz-covered chair with my legs tucked under me and my lap covered with a soft, well-worn quilt.

For a time, I simply sat there, listening to the rain, my eyes closed. Then I began to pray, using a passage from Romans I'd memorized.

"Therefore, since I've been made right in God's sight by faith, I have peace with God because of what Jesus Christ my Lord has done for me. Because of my faith, Christ has brought me into this place of highest privilege where I now stand, and I confidently and joyfully look forward to sharing God's glory."

I paused at this point, as I always did when I used this prayer, and focused my mind on the words. I longed to see them manifested in my life.

"I can rejoice, too, when I run into problems and trials, for I know that they're good for me—they help me learn to endure. And endurance develops strength of character in me, and character strengthens my confident expectation of salvation. And this expectation will not disappoint me."

I drew my closed Bible tight against my chest, hugging it, allowing myself to feel God hugging me.

"For I know how dearly God loves me, because He's given me the Holy Spirit to fill my heart with His love. Amen."

I drew a deep breath.

Problems and trials are good for me because they teach me to endure. But, Father, I'm tired. Is there never to be an end to the trials? Must I forever endure? Am I never to be happy in my marriage?

I opened my eyes, gazing toward the rain-spattered window, a little surprised by my own thoughts. I'd kept them at arm's length for weeks now, not allowing them to form consciously, not wanting to face them.

"I think he's drinking again."

The words cut me like a knife, slashing at my heart.

"O God, not again."

Still clutching my Bible to my chest, I rose from the chair, the hand-stitched quilt falling into a multicolored puddle on the floor at my feet. I stepped over it and walked to the window, where I pressed my forehead against the cool glass. The world, as seen through the rain-streaked window, was a distorted blur.

Rather like I felt . . . distorted and blurred.

In the past five years, Gideon had promised many times that he'd taken his last drink, that he wouldn't do it anymore, that he would change. And again and again, he'd broken his promises to me.

Why, God? Why?

I'd believed Gideon . . . again. He'd shown resolve for a number of months. I'd thought this time he would succeed, that this time he would keep his promise. But I'd also thought he would succeed the time before that . . . and the time before that . . . and the time before that.

"I'm so naive. I'm such a fool."

Deep in a secret corner of my heart, I wished I could hate Gideon. If I hated him, he couldn't hurt me. Right? I was so tired of being hurt.

How long, O Lord? How long?

Those words stirred something inside me. I straightened away from the window and opened my Bible. I flipped through the pages until I found the verses I sought.

I am sick at heart. How long, O Lord, until You restore me? Return, O Lord, and rescue me. Save me because of Your unfailing love.

"Jesus, I'm sick at heart. Restore me. Rescue me because of Your love."

I am worn out from sobbing. Every night tears drench my bed; my pillow is wet from weeping. My vision is blurred by grief.

"I'm like David, Father. My pillow is drenched by tears." I choked back a sob and once again leaned my forehead against the window. "I'm so tired of crying. I'm so tired of the fear."

The fears. They seemed endless. I was afraid of what others

would say. I was afraid about money—or the lack thereof. I was afraid Gideon would hurt himself. I was afraid he might hurt someone else.

Not that Gideon was ever violent. Oh, no. Just the opposite. When he drank, he withdrew, pulled inside himself, grew morose. He turned away from me and the children. Sharon Rose and Peter were too little to notice much yet, but I noticed. Oh, how I noticed.

"I'm so alone, Father. I'm tired of being married but alone."

What was my greatest fear? That I would get my wish. That I would grow to hate him even more than I hated his drinking.

Hate the sin but love the sinner. Isn't that what they said at church?

How trite. How impossible.

The rain fell harder, spattering the glass. If only it could wash away my fears of the future.

"Why can't he stop? Why can't he see what he's doing to us? Why is he so selfish?"

I didn't like Gideon when he drank. And I didn't like myself when he drank either.

I didn't like myself when I pretended to step close for a kiss when what I really wanted was to smell his breath. I didn't like myself when I conducted frantic searches through drawers and cupboards, looking for one of his bottles. I didn't like myself when I listened to Gideon speak, not to hear what he said but to judge how he said it. I didn't like myself when I treated Gideon like a child instead of a man. I didn't like the sharpness of my tongue, the cruel things I could say in a flash. Most of all, I didn't like my lack of faith. I could believe God for anything— anything except Gideon's sobriety.

Images of my husband at his worst—intoxicated, stumbling, fumbling, incoherent, made stupid by drink—raced through my mind. I squeezed my eyes closed, trying to block them out. It was at that moment, into the horrid turmoil of my heart and head, that God spoke.

"For I hate divorce!" says the Lord, the God of Israel.

I held my breath, struck instantly with the certain understanding that God wasn't speaking those words as a warning or a reprimand but instead was giving them to me as a promise.

And yet, if Gideon was drinking again—

Believe and don't doubt, beloved.

"Believe and don't doubt," I echoed softly. "I'll try, Father. I'll try."

Janelle Burns and her son, Joshua, came for a visit that same afternoon.

Janelle had become my best and truest friend through the years. She was my only constant confidante besides the Lord, the only person I had allowed to see inside the hidden corners of my heart.

I couldn't share the details of our marriage with my parents. I'd learned that they held grudges against Gideon for hurting me even while I was doing my best to forgive him. I'd tried to hide those times when Gideon started drinking again, but I hadn't always succeeded. Mother had even encouraged me once to bring the children and go live with them. "No one would blame you, dear, if you divorced him."

I'd talked some to Pastor Clyde, and while I was certain he wouldn't hold a grudge as my parents did, I still kept my deepest hurts to myself.

So it was only Janelle Burns who understood fully the reality of my life. She understood, not only because I told her things I told no one else but because she, too, loved an alcoholic.

Alcoholic. Even now I recoiled from the word. It made me feel ashamed, a failure. What was wrong with me that Gideon couldn't stop drinking? If I was a good wife, if he loved me enough, surely he would stop. Surely he would see what he was doing to himself and to me. Surely . . .

I shook off the troubling thoughts as I stepped onto the porch, holding Peter in my arms so he wouldn't run into the driveway before my friend parked her car.

"Joshua!" Sharon Rose squealed, then jumped up and down, waving madly.

The Burnses had adopted their son two years before, when Joshua was almost three years old. Their miracle child, they called him. Blind from birth and abandoned by his unwed teenage mother, Joshua had lived in an institution until he was taken home by Janelle and Ted. Every other Monday for more than a year, Janelle had brought her son out to our farm to play with Sharon Rose and Peter. Sometimes I wondered if Joshua was an excuse, if Janelle came more for me than for him.

I descended the porch steps, thankful the day had turned to one of blue skies and sunshine.

"How are you?" Janelle called as she got out of her car.

"Good. And you?"

"Great." She opened the back door and helped Joshua to the ground.

I set Peter on his feet and he and Sharon Rose ran to greet their friend.

"I made iced tea," I said. "Want some?"

"You bet."

"Sharon Rose, you and your brother take Joshua into the backyard. And play nice, all of you."

"We will, Mommy."

Janelle settled onto the back porch, where she could keep an eye on the children while I went inside for our beverages. A short while later, I sat beside her, cold glass in hand.

"How was your Mother's Day?" Janelle asked me.

"Very nice. Pastor Clyde preached a wonderful sermon, and all the mothers in the congregation went home with flowers. How about yours?" I sipped tea from my glass.

"After church Ted took me to Sunday brunch at the Royal. He arranged for a sitter for Joshua and everything. We sat and talked for the longest time." The sparkle of love in her eyes was unmistakable.

I felt a sting of envy.

"Deborah?"

There was no point in trying to hide my thoughts from Janelle. She knew me too well. "I think Gideon's started drinking again."

Pained understanding crossed her face. "Oh."

"I don't have any proof," I added. "He's become an expert at hiding it from me. It's just something I feel."

"Have you spoken to him? Have you asked him outright?"

I shook my head. "What good would it do? He'd say it isn't true, and I couldn't contradict him. I haven't found any empty bottles or smelled alcohol on his breath. All I've got is this . . . this instinct telling me. But if it *is* true, if he's drinking and he says he isn't, then he'll be lying to me."

Again. Lying to me again.

I turned my head, staring at the barn. "Is that any way to run a marriage, to accuse one's husband of being a liar?"

Janelle laid a hand on my shoulder.

"Why does he do it?" I whispered.

"Willie told me once that if it were just willpower that was needed to quit, he would have stopped long before he got into trouble. Even as young as he was at the time, he knew he was hurting the family. He didn't want to hurt us or anybody else. He knew he'd lost control." She took a deep breath, then added, "Last time I visited Willie in prison, he told me he knows he would go right back to drinking when he gets out if God hadn't taken ahold of him there."

My gaze was drawn to Janelle. "But Gideon's been a Christian for years. Why hasn't that made a difference in him?"

"Christians fall into sin whenever we don't walk in obedience. You know what I'm saying is true." She leaned toward me. "Deborah, I tried so hard to control my brother's actions. I wore myself out trying to control him. I screamed and I cajoled and I cried. But the truth is I couldn't control him. I can't control anything. I make a very poor Holy Spirit. I haven't the wisdom or the power or the grace. I needed to get out of God's way and let Him work. I had to turn Willie over to the Lord, even if it meant letting him fall into the pit. And then I had to surrender myself to God's will, too, whatever that might be. That's the only place I could find peace."

But what about me and the children? What if Gideon doesn't stop drinking? What happens to us then?

Bernice Richardson

Lately, I couldn't say a word to my daughter about her husband. If there was even the slightest inflection of disapproval in my voice, she shut me out.

I wondered sometimes if she simply didn't see what her father and I saw.

I wanted her to be happy. What mother doesn't want that for her child? I didn't understand why all that had to happen to her. Not then. Not now. Deborah was loving, caring, giving. She didn't deserve that sort of worry, the kind Gideon gave her. Wasn't it enough she lost her first husband so tragically?

Oh, I suppose I was being unfair, but I couldn't seem to help myself. I knew Gideon had good qualities. Or he had at one time. I couldn't say I saw many of them anymore.

As for Deborah, she was much too thin. My goodness, I packed on an extra fifteen pounds after she was born and never did manage to lose them. But my daughter was thinner than the day she graduated from high school. Of course, chasing after two little ones while running a household can wear any woman down—even one as strong willed as Deborah.

I wished she wouldn't insist on remaining at the farm with Gideon. We would've let her and the children move in with us. We told her so.

CHAPTER THIRTY-FIVE

I was mistaken.

I stared through the screen door, watching as Gideon led Boone around the corral, the children on the gelding's back, both of them fit snugly in the seat of the saddle. Sharon Rose giggled at something her father said; then Peter echoed her laughter. The merry sound was music to my ears.

He's fine. We're all fine.

As if hearing my thoughts, Gideon looked toward the house, saw me, and waved.

I stepped onto the porch. "Lunch is ready. Come in and eat."

"Not yet, Mommy," Sharon Rose said in a pleading tone.

"Not yet, Mommy," Peter mimicked.

Gideon called, "Not yet, Mommy," and he sounded just like the children.

"Well . . . " I had a hard time not laughing. "I suppose Heidi would like these sandwiches if you don't want them, but I'm not sure she'll care for the chocolate chip cookies."

"Chocolate chip cookies?" Gideon scooped Sharon Rose and Peter from the saddle and set them on the ground. "We can't let Heidi have our cookies." He gave each of their bottoms a light swat, talking loudly enough so I could hear him. "Hurry, you two, and save my place at the table." He straightened, his grin bright. "I'll be right in, Deb, soon as I take care of Boone."

"I promise not to let Heidi take your food." I opened the screen door as the children scrambled up the porch steps. "Wash your hands and faces first." They raced for the bathroom, Sharon Rose in the lead.

My heart was feeling a good deal lighter than it had been only a few days before. I wondered now why I'd been in such a blue funk. Obviously I'd been wrong about everything.

Sounding like a thundering herd of buffalo, Sharon Rose and Peter returned to the kitchen, their faces damp and shiny.

"Let me see your hands." I inspected the pudgy limbs that were immediately extended toward me. "Good job."

I lifted Peter into the high chair, then slid it close to the table. Recently, our son had begun complaining about the high chair, protesting he wasn't a baby and didn't need it. I wanted to tell him not to be in such a hurry to grow up. I wanted to tell him he would be grown much too soon anyway.

Sharon Rose climbed onto the kitchen chair opposite her brother. Gideon had made a small booster seat for her. Without it, her chin barely cleared the tabletop.

I brought a platter of tuna salad sandwiches to the table, then filled each child's glass with cold milk from the Frigidaire.

By the time I'd put the pitcher back into the refrigerator, Gideon had arrived.

"Hurry, Daddy, and wash up," Sharon Rose said, "before Heidi gets your sandwich." She covered her mouth with her hand as she giggled.

Gideon and I exchanged proud-parent glances.

"I'll hurry. I'm starved." He disappeared down the hall.

I took my seat and placed my napkin in my lap. Seeing me, the children did the same. Moments later, Gideon reappeared and sat at the head of the table.

We exchanged another glance; then we all held hands and Gideon blessed the food. A quick and perfunctory prayer, perhaps, but a blessing all the same.

"I'm going over to Merle's after lunch. He asked me to help make some repairs to his barn. You and the kids want to come along?"

I smiled, pleased to be asked, but shook my head. "I've got laundry to do. I've been putting it off because of the rainy weather, but now that it's stopped I can't put it off another day." I handed him the platter of sandwiches. "Besides, the children will need to lie down for their naps."

Sharon Rose said, "I don't need a nap, Mommy. I'm getting too big."

"We're never too big to take naps, sugar." Gideon reached over to ruffle her dark curls. "Wouldn't mind one myself, come to think of it."

Truly, I don't know why I'd doubted Gideon. He was fine.

Reluctant though they were, the children fell asleep not long after I put them down. I immediately filled the pockets of my apron with clothespins, took the clean wash from the machine, dropping it into a large basket, then carried the basket outside to hang the clothes on the line.

Heidi stayed on the porch and watched me with soulful brown eyes while listening for the children. The role of protector was one my faithful dog had assumed as soon as Sharon Rose started to crawl.

Softly I said, "I don't know how I'd keep track of them without your help, Heidi."

As if knowing I was talking to her, even from that distance, she lifted her head, ears cocked forward.

I smiled and reached for another article of clothing in the basket.

The sun was pleasantly warm upon my back, and the air was sweet, still fresh after the rain that had come to us in waves for several days. Soon enough, I would be complaining about the heat and the long dry spells, but not today. Today I relished the sun and the clear skies.

After hanging the last item from the basket, I glanced toward the porch. Heidi had lowered her head to her paws, indicating there were no sounds of mischief coming from inside the house. This was a good opportunity to check the feed bins in the barn. Tomorrow was Friday, the day I drove the truck into Amethyst for groceries and farm supplies. I didn't want to forget anything.

I left the wicker basket on the ground and strolled toward the barn, my thoughts drifting to the summer Gideon repaired its sagging roof. How long ago that seemed to me now, and yet how like yesterday. Strange, the way one's mind perceives time.

Daniel and Boone trotted across the pasture, no doubt hoping for a handful of grain or a sugar cube.

"Why should I give you anything?" I asked them when they

reached the fence. "In the old days, you'd have to work for your keep, pulling the plow or a wagon. You two are just a couple of pets, like Heidi." I stroked the white star on Daniel's forehead, then patted Boone's neck. "You'll have to wait for a treat. My pockets are empty."

Daniel snorted, as if in disgust.

I laughed aloud, turned on my heel, and walked into the barn, squinting to see in the dim light.

We could use that bigger barn, I thought as I opened the door to the feed-and-tack room. But a new barn would take more money than we had, even if Gideon and I did all the labor ourselves.

I checked the feed bins. They were low, but my experienced eye told me we could wait another week before replenishing. That was good news since our bank account was on the lean side at the moment. But Gideon expected a check to arrive by Monday for carpentry work he'd done over in Nampa, and that would see us through for a while.

I could almost hear my mother saying, *I don't know why you stay there, Deborah. No one can ever get ahead with a farm the size of yours. Even I know that.*

I knew it, too. I'd always known it. But money wasn't the point. There were so many other reasons—good reasons—for us to choose this life. I liked the country, and I liked our neighbors and our church. I liked the slower pace. The children were happy here, too. We did without some things, but not anything that mattered.

And I feel safer here. My pulse quickened. *Am I safer here?*

My gaze slid over the shelves and bins and paraphernalia that filled this small, dusty, leather-smelling room.

God, am I safer here?

What possessed me to open the lid to the nearest feed bin a second time? What possessed me to reach down inside and run my hand through the grain in a round, sweeping motion? And when I found nothing but grain, what possessed me to repeat the action in the second bin and then in the third?

And how could I possibly describe what I felt when I pulled the half-empty vodka bottle from the deepest, farthest corner of the fourth?

— *Merle Johnson* —

My brother's boy, Richard, had come to stay with us for the summer. He said he wanted to try his hand at dairy farming, see if it was the life for him.

Course, Richard wasn't a boy. He was a man of thirty-five. About the same age as Gideon Clermont, give or take a year on either side. Richard had himself a rough time in his teens and twenties. Got himself into some regular scrapes. My brother, he kept the details real close to his vest, even with his own kin. Still, I surmised Richard, as a teenager, single-handedly turned his dad's hair stone gray.

Thank the good Lord there wasn't anything of that troublemaker left in Richard. My missus wouldn't've put up with any shenanigans. But she didn't have to worry. Richard was as steady as a rock, a deep thinker, a man of deep moral and religious convictions, and right pleasant company, if truth be told.

That day, working on the dairy barn, was the first time my neighbor Gideon and Richard met. Me being the old fellow on the repair crew, I let them do the climbing around on the high places, meaning they spent several hours working side by side, out of my hearing. I figured they talked some.

Anyway, after Gideon left, Richard made a strange comment. Something about how being with Gideon was like looking into a mirror. I told him I didn't think the two of them looked anything alike.

Richard, he just shook his head as he walked inside the house.

CHAPTER THIRTY-SIX

I simmered and seethed all afternoon. I wanted to confront Gideon the instant he returned from the Johnson farm. By an act of will, I managed to hold my tongue until after the children had gone to bed for the night. But as soon as they were settled and I knew they were asleep, I went looking for Gideon. I found him near the corral. Returning, no doubt, from visiting another stash inside the barn.

"Are you intoxicated yet?" I asked.

"What?"

"How much have you had to drink today? Will you be drunk by bedtime?"

"Where'd you get the idea I'm drinking?"

I pulled the vodka bottle from the back pocket of my Levi's. "This is where I got the idea."

"I don't know where that came from."

"Don't lie to me, Gideon. I'm so tired of the lies."

His eyes narrowed and his mouth thinned.

"I found it in the barn where you hid it."

"Where?"

"Why do you want me to tell you? So you can find a new hiding spot? You promised me you weren't going to drink anymore. After the last time, you promised me."

It frightened me, the fury that swept over me, through me, consuming me. It was a white-hot rage that filled every capillary, every pore, every muscle, every bone in my body. I wanted to hurl something at him. I wanted to hurt him, make him feel a little bit of the pain I felt. I nearly gave into the desire. I nearly hit him with that vodka bottle.

"You're being unfair." Gideon sounded indignant. "Who knows how old that bottle is?"

For a moment, doubt surfaced. What if I was wrong? What if this *was* an old bottle? But then I looked into his eyes, saw his defensiveness, and I knew. I *knew*.

"What a fool I am," I whispered. "What an unmitigated fool."

I spun on my heel and headed for the house. Halfway there, Gideon's hand on my arm stopped me.

"Be reasonable, Deb." He tightened his grip, no doubt because of the stubborn set of my jaw and the stiff nonresponsiveness of my body.

"*Reasonable?* Don't you understand anything? I hate what you're doing to us. I hate it!"

He released me, took a step backward.

I stared at him—this man who was the father of my children, this man who'd made me smile again and laugh again and love again—and I knew he could see my loathing.

Was it loathing for the drink itself or for the man who drank? I wasn't sure.

God, I can't take it. I can't take it anymore.

The rage drained from me, and all that was left was emptiness, hopelessness, complete and total defeat.

"You're never going to change," I said, my voice flat.

"Deb—"

I held up my hand like a traffic cop. "Don't! Don't say anything, Gideon. I don't want to hear anything you have to say."

This time when I headed for the house, he let me go.

———

I lay on the bed, the darkness of night filling the bedroom. I was dry-eyed. There were no tears left in me to weep. My heart was like sawdust. I knew I should pray. There was a part of me that *wanted* to pray. But in prayer, I was supposed to believe for God's answer, and I was fresh out of faith. I couldn't believe in anything tonight. Not anything.

I knew what was coming next. Gideon would withdraw more and more. He would suffer from the "flu" more often. He would have headaches and body aches. He would find excuses why he couldn't go with me to church functions or to the neighbors'. He would forget things, suffer blackouts. At some point, he wouldn't be able to hide his condition from me. He wouldn't be able to lie his way out. I would say horrible things, worse even than what I'd said today. But it wouldn't matter much because he would be too drunk to hear or understand. And the next day he would make promises. Always the promises. For a time he would keep them. Maybe for a day. Maybe for a week. Maybe for a few months. Maybe even for a year. But then it would all begin again. It *always* began again.

"I hate divorce!" says the Lord.

I clutched a pillow to my chest, and like Jacob, I wrestled with God.

"I thought it was a promise, but it's a sentence. What wrong have I done to deserve this? What wrong have my children done? I can't bear it. It isn't fair. I can't take it. I can't!"

I heard noises from downstairs. Gideon fumbling around in the kitchen.

One of these days he would probably fall down the stairs and break his neck.

And I'll bet he wouldn't have the decency to die if he did fall. I'd be stuck caring for him for the rest of my life.

I felt sick to my stomach, sickened that I could think such a thing.

O Jesus, what if he's never okay? What if he continues down this road? What if—

I started to weep then, silently, tears streaming down my cheeks.

— *Sophie* —

I've served drinks in places like this for most of my adult life. I know all the types of drinkers who pass through the doors of beer joints and cocktail lounges and smoky bar and grills. They come looking for some magic potion to shut out the noise in their heads and the pain in their lives. It ain't long before I can tell how far down the road to perdition any one of my customers has traveled.

That guy, I'd never seen him before. But one look in his eyes told me he'd just about reached the beginning of the end. I figured he still had a wife or somebody who cared for him. His clothes were clean, and he didn't look like he'd been without a decent meal in a year or more, the way some do. It was coming hard on him, the end, but he wasn't there yet.

I'll make it clear to you, right up front. I ain't no saint and I ain't out to rescue nobody. If I was, I sure wouldn't't've been working in a windowless dump like that one, stuck out on the Owyhee Desert in the middle of nowhere. That was the kind of place where people come *not* to be seen by the folks who know them, and so I respected that. Live and let live. That's my motto.

Still, there was something about that guy that made me want to tell him to go home while he still had one to go to. *Go home to that pretty little wife of yours, mister.* That's what I wanted to say.

I wanted to, but I didn't. I served him that screwdriver he ordered and I wondered where he'd be come closing time.

CHAPTER THIRTY-SEVEN

Gideon and I didn't speak to each other for several days. At least nothing beyond the unavoidable "excuse me" and "pass the potatoes, please."

My emotions fluctuated wildly—sometimes from minute to minute—between total detachment and an anger so hot it threatened to consume me utterly.

I hated him.

I loved him.

I wanted him out.

I wanted him well.

I'd run out of strength.

I'd run out of wisdom.

I was at the end of my rope.

I was at the end of my hope.

Which, of course, was exactly where God was waiting.

— Richard Johnson —

It isn't easy to love an alcoholic. Ask anybody who does.

Alcoholics lie to the people who love us, and depending upon how far gone we are, we've probably done much worse than tell lies. I know I did in my drinking days. I had a boatload of wrongs to make amends for, I'll tell you that.

The thing is, the first place an alcoholic needs to find fellowship and forgiveness, if he hopes to break free of his addiction and be restored to a place of respect and dignity, is in the home—from the very people he's hurt the most.

I'd been sober eight years by the time I met Gideon. It had been eight years since I woke up in a strange town in a strange hotel and had no idea what day it was or how I got there. Eight years since a man from a local mission had put his arm around my shoulders and shared the plan of salvation with me and got me started down the road to recovery.

I won't lie to you. Asking Jesus to come live in my heart didn't make a life of sobriety a cakewalk. I had to make it one day at a time. There were many occasions when I fought the desire to drink, many whispered thoughts like *You can handle just one.* The difference was, now I knew where to turn when those temptations came. It was only God who could restore me to sanity and keep me sane.

I remembered what it was like when I went home to see my parents. That was about six months after I got sober. I guess I was fortunate never to have married during my drinking years. I hadn't hurt a wife and kids the way many others have. But my folks . . . oh, man.

When I went home, I could see how hard it was for them to believe I'd really changed. That took time, and I had to accept it was going to take however long it took

and not one minute less. I didn't destroy their trust overnight, and I wasn't going to get it back overnight either.

It wasn't until after I returned to college and then graduated that my dad said he figured *maybe* I really wasn't going
to start drinking again. It took four years before he even
began to hope I *might* stay sober. I guess that tells you how
much I hurt him.

After getting my business degree, I received a good job
offer with a large multinational corporation. I'm sure my
dad thought I'd gone off the deep end again when I turned
it down. It was hard to explain to him, but I felt God wanted
me to do something else with my life. The problem was,
I didn't know what the something else might be.

I won't bore you with the details about how I ended up
on my uncle's dairy farm for the summer. I'm not sure how
it came about myself. I'd become accustomed to heeding the
quiet voice of God in my heart when I heard it and trusting
He would reveal what I needed to know when I needed to
know it.

As soon as I met Gideon Clermont, I knew the reason
God had brought me to Amethyst.

CHAPTER THIRTY-EIGHT

Love Gideon, God told me. *Forgive him.*

How could I? How could I love and forgive when he wouldn't even *try* to get well? How could I love and forgive when he was treating me and the children so carelessly?

With My help, came the Lord's answer.

But it wasn't fair. Why should *I* be the one who had to forgive?

Because He had called me to forgive seventy times seven. Because He had called me to love and forgive people while they were yet in sin.

But forgive Gideon while he was still drinking? It was too hard. Too hard.

Whenever trouble comes your way, let it be an opportunity for joy. That's what the Bible said.

This? An opportunity for joy?

My marriage was an unhappy one. My children scarcely saw their father—and too often when they did, I wished they didn't have to because that meant he was probably passed out on the sofa or stumbling around in the kitchen. Gideon seemed bent on total self-destruction, and he was doing it right before our eyes.

How could I consider any of this joyful? It wasn't humanly possible!

Not humanly, beloved, God whispered into my heart. *But with Me, all things are possible. Even this.*

But Gideon—the Gideon I knew today—was no longer the man I'd married. He'd changed. Changed too much. This wasn't the life I was supposed to have. Why me? Why was this happening to me?

Why not you, beloved?

Why not me? Because I didn't deserve it.

Did My Son deserve the cross?

Oh, how that thought pierced my heart. Jesus hadn't deserved the cross, but He'd gone willingly. For me. He'd gone willingly for me.

And the question was, what was I willing to do for Him? Could I love and forgive Gideon for Jesus' sake if not for my own?

On a hot afternoon in late May, with the temperature climbing past ninety degrees, I found myself sitting on the covered patio of Janelle Burns's south Boise home while the children entertained themselves in the sandbox. Speaking softly, I told Janelle everything that had transpired since her last visit to the farm.

"If Mother knew what was going on," I finished at long last, "she would demand I leave him immediately. She would order me to move in with her and Dad. She's hinted at it countless times . . ."

Janelle watched me intently. "Do you *want* to leave Gideon?"

"No." I paused, shook my head. "Yes. Sometimes." I sighed. "I don't know. I'm confused."

Janelle didn't say anything. She was good at waiting.

I glanced at my hands, folded tightly in my lap. "God wants me to love and forgive Gideon. I know that." I drew in a shaky breath. "He wants me to consider it all joy. Even this."

"Mmm."

"I don't know if I can. I don't know what I feel half the time. I'm so afraid of what tomorrow will bring."

"Deborah, there's a prayer I think might help you. Willie sent it to me from prison. God has used it to bring me a great deal of comfort. Let me give you a copy before you leave. Try reading it every morning during your devotional time, and then ask God to give you wisdom, to show you what you're supposed to do in the days and weeks to come. He promises to give us wisdom whenever we ask, as long as we ask in faith."

The truth was, I didn't want a prayer to recite. I wanted an answer right then. I didn't want to wait, to pray, to trust. I wanted to be rescued. *Now!*

As if she'd heard my thoughts, Janelle said, "Sometimes God takes us out of our problems, but most of the time, He walks us through them. It's part of the learning process of life."

Whenever trouble comes your way, let it be an opportunity for joy.

I imagined myself, much the way I might see Sharon Rose when she was defiant, stomping my foot and jutting out my chin toward God and crying, *"No!"*

"Deborah?"

I met Janelle's gaze.

"Do you believe God is omnipotent, that He's ultimately in control?"

I frowned. "Of course I do."

"Then you need to relinquish Gideon to Him."

"I have."

"Have you?" She leaned forward on her chair. "You want Gideon to be honest with you, to not tell you any more lies. That's understandable. Now you need to be honest with yourself as well. If God is in control, doesn't that mean nothing comes into your life that isn't allowed there by God Himself?" She reached out, covering my folded hands with one of hers. "While we're here on earth, we're constantly being tested and refined."

Refined. Is that what was happening? Was I in the midst of God's refining fire? If so, it wasn't where I wanted to be. I wanted out! It was too hot, too painful.

I rose from my chair. "I'd better get home or I'll never have dinner ready in time."

"I'm always here for you, Deborah. Any time at all." She gave me a hug. "I'll go get a copy of that prayer for you." She disappeared inside the house.

"Sharon Rose. Peter. Come on. It's time to go home."

"We don't wanna go," Sharon Rose protested.

"Well, you have to anyway. Come along. Be good now."

After some feet dragging and pleading looks from the children, I managed to get most of the sand brushed off their clothes, and by the time I had them settled onto the backseat of the Nash, Janelle arrived, a folded slip of paper in her hand.

She gave it to me, saying, "I think this will bless you, Deborah."

"Thanks." I shoved the paper into my pocketbook as I headed for the driver's side door.

"Call me. Any time you need to."

I felt a warning sting of tears. "I will." I got into the car, stuck the key into the switch, and turned it. The engine came to life, and with a wave of my right hand in Janelle's direction, I pulled away from the curb.

It wasn't long before I'd left suburbia behind. A straight ribbon of deserted country road lay before me. The children grew quiet; I knew without looking they'd fallen asleep.

Oh, to be able to do that. To simply trust that Mommy would get them safely home and so fall off to sleep in peace.

"But who will get me safely home?" I whispered. "O Jesus, I'm afraid. I don't know what to do."

On the heels of my pitiful prayer came a passage of Scripture, the one Janelle had referred to earlier: *If you need wisdom—if you want to know what God wants you to do—ask Him, and He will gladly tell you. He will not resent your asking.*

Perhaps therein lay the problem. Did I *want* to know what God wanted me to do? Perhaps not. Not if it wasn't what I wanted for myself.

— *Pastor Clyde Beekman* —

I failed the Clermonts in many ways during those first five years. I failed because of my ignorance regarding alcohol addiction. One can learn only so much from books. The rest takes experience.

I wasn't the only one who failed them. The church did, too. The church is the place the alcoholic and his family should feel welcome, but a congregation doesn't always react as they should when they learn there's a drinking problem with one of its members. Too often people treat the alcoholic as if he's weak willed. I've learned that's erroneous. In fact, the opposite is true. His will may be distorted, but it isn't weak.

Gideon came to my office once, nearly two years ago. I realize now he was reaching out for help. But I couldn't read the signs at the time, and my lack of understanding failed him.

But despite all of the things I didn't understand at the time, this much I knew without question: God *loved* Gideon Clermont. God was *for* Gideon Clermont and wanted him whole and well and walking in obedience to Him.

Gideon wouldn't get well until he desired God's will more than he wanted his own. I wanted that desire to take hold of Gideon's heart. I prayed the Lord would show me how to be of service to my brother in Christ, how to help set him free from his bondage before it killed him.

CHAPTER THIRTY-NINE

God, grant me the serenity
to accept the things I cannot change,
the courage to change the things I can,
and the wisdom to know the difference.
Living one day at a time,
enjoying one moment at a time,
accepting hardship as a pathway to peace;
taking, as Jesus did, this sinful world as it is,
not as I would have it;
trusting that You will make all things right
if I surrender to Your will;
so that I may be reasonably happy in this life
and supremely happy with You
forever in the next. Amen.

—REINHOLD NIEBUHR

Janelle was right. The prayer brought comfort. It challenged me to keep seeking God's wisdom and to surrender all—Gideon, our marriage, myself—to Him.

As I sought God's will with a new fervency, something changed within me. I began to pray for Gideon in a new way, no longer asking God to change my husband so that *I* might be happy and secure. I caught a glimpse of how selfish my heart was when I prayed in that manner. Now I tried to pray for Gideon for Gideon's sake alone.

Well, almost for his sake alone.

But the harder I prayed, the more Gideon's life seemed to spiral out of control. The more I prayed, the sicker he seemed to get, the more he seemed to drink, the further away from me he pulled.

I can see now how reluctant the enemy was to let go. For we were not fighting against people made of flesh and blood, but against the evil rulers and authorities of the unseen world, against those mighty powers of darkness, and against wicked spirits in the heavenly realms.

Dust and chaff floated on the still afternoon air. The steady growl of the mowing machine as it moved through the alfalfa fields, cutting the first crop of the season, reached my ears. I paused where I stood, raised a hand to shield my eyes from the glare of the sun, and looked toward the far end of our property.

Father God, make Gideon hungry for You and for Your Word. Make his appetite for You greater than his appetite for anything else. Don't let him find satisfaction in anything or anyone until he has found it in You.

Lowering my hand from my eyes, I took hold of the rug I'd

set down on the railing and gave it another good shake before turning toward the house. I stopped when I saw a man—a stranger—walking up our driveway. He was tall with broad shoulders and pale blond—almost white—hair.

"Hello," he called. "Are you Deborah Clermont?"

Heidi came off the porch to stand between me and our visitor.

"Yes," I answered. "I'm Mrs. Clermont."

"I'm Richard Johnson." He motioned behind him. "I'm working for my uncle Merle."

I smiled then. "Oh, yes. Your aunt Gertrude told me you were here for the summer. Welcome."

"Thanks." He stopped a few paces on the other side of Heidi. "I came over to see if I could lend your husband a hand."

"That's kind of you, Mr. Johnson."

He grinned. "To be honest, I needed a change of scenery. I'm tired of looking at cows. I haven't seen Gideon since the day he helped repair the roof on Uncle Merle's barn, so I thought it'd be nice to come chew the fat with him." He looked past me toward the field. "How's he doing?"

What was Richard asking? What did he mean? Had Gideon done something I didn't know about?

"Mind if I go on out there?" Richard asked.

I felt my tension ease; he was just being neighborly.

"No. Go right ahead."

I watched as Richard strode across the barnyard and into the back acreage. I had the oddest feeling of . . . of what? Hope? Expectation? Change? I wasn't sure, but—

"Mommy!"

It's difficult to think deep thoughts when one is the mother of a four-year-old.

I turned toward the house. My daughter stood on the porch, the front of her clothes stained purple.

"What happened, Sharon Rose?"

"I spilled the Kool-Aid."

I swallowed a groan. I'd waxed the kitchen floor not more than half an hour ago. "Why didn't you call for Mommy before you tried to pour yourself a drink? You know that pitcher is too heavy for you."

She rubbed her eyes with her fists. "I'm sorry." She made a pitiful sight.

"Don't cry, honey. It's all right. Let's go clean it up, shall we? Then we can change your clothes, and afterward, we'll make a new pitcher of Kool-Aid to have with our dinner. Okay?"

I heard men's voices and went to stand at the open door. Through the screen I saw them, walking side by side, companionable, like old friends. I felt a sting of longing for the days when Gideon and I had strolled together like that, our steps unhurried, simply enjoying each other's company.

Drawing a deep breath, I pushed open the screen door. "Finished for the day?"

"Yes," Gideon answered, sounding more like himself than he had in a long while.

"Dinner's ready. Are you hungry?"

"Starved."

I looked toward Richard. "Would you like to stay and eat with us, Mr. Johnson? There's plenty, and it's the least we can do to repay you for your kindness."

"As a matter of fact, I'd like that a lot. If you're sure it's no bother."

Gideon answered before I could, "We're sure." He motioned toward the pump near the corner of the house. "We'll wash up out here."

It had been a long while since Gideon had a friend. A close friend, as Janelle was to me. Not since Norm Adams. Not since we'd moved back to the farm. It shouldn't be that way. Gideon was likeable really . . .

When he was himself . . .

When he wasn't drinking.

But these days, Gideon didn't let anybody get close to him. He withdrew, put up walls, shut himself away.

Just as he's done with me.

No, I wasn't going to walk down the path of self-pity today. I was going to rejoice in my blessings. I was going to be grateful to God.

As I rearranged the table, making room for another chair and another place setting, I began a mental list of all the things I was thankful for. I was thankful Gideon was in good spirits today. I was thankful my children were healthy and happy. I was thankful the first cutting of hay would be plentiful. I was thankful for all the Lord was teaching me.

As the list grew in my mind, I began to hum "Blessed Assurance," not aware I was doing so until a deep male voice joined in.

"This is my story, this is my song, praising my Savior all the day long."

I turned and met Richard's gaze as he entered the kitchen, still singing the hymn. He smiled as he finished the last refrain.

The kitchen fell absolutely silent for several heartbeats. Then Gideon said, "Sounds like you were trying out for the church choir, Rich."

"No. I just love to praise the Lord. Singing makes my heart glad."

So that was why I'd felt hope when I met Richard. He was a believer.

"Mr. Johnson, if you'll sit there," I said, pointing, "on Gideon's left, I'll get the children and we can begin."

Sharon Rose and Peter were both well behaved throughout the meal. No milk was spilled. No chairs tipped over. No teasing and torturing each other. It was bliss.

I admit, I was sorry when dinner was finished and Richard bid us a good evening. I was sorry to see him go. For while he was there, we'd seemed like a normal, happy family.

After he left, Gideon said he had chores to do in the barn. I knew he wouldn't come to bed for a long, long time.

Mary Margaret Foster

I wouldn't see my fiftieth year again. Having reached the mature age that I had, you'd think I'd've learned a thing or two about the way things are, about human nature and all. But I have to be honest. I didn't believe Gideon Clermont was a hard-drinking man.

First time I heard that gossip from Alice Gordon—that would be a couple of years ago at least—I all but called her a liar straight to her face. I found it so absurd.

I've known a few drunks in my day. They're mean and dirty, most of them. Like the hobos who ride the rails or the men who live in shantytowns and don't have two nickels to rub together.

Gideon Clermont, on the other hand, was a family man. I've seen him with his wife and kids, and it was clear as anything that he was good to them. He farmed his land and worked odd jobs. He was always clean and well mannered when he came into our store.

But come to think of it, about the time that talk started up again, he wasn't coming in as often as he used to.

Anyway, as I was saying, I didn't believe the gossip the first time I heard it. But the rumors persisted. You know how small towns are. Impossible to keep most things private.

CHAPTER FORTY

Giggles and high-pitched squeals filled the air as Sharon Rose and Peter took turns darting through the sprinkler. Heidi lay in the shade of the big willow tree, keeping a vigilant watch while at the same time staying out of water's reach.

The innocence of youth.

My jaw clenched, a reflex action, as anger welled inside me.

Last night, while I washed the dinner dishes, Sharon Rose had come into the kitchen and tugged at my apron.

"Something's wrong with Daddy," she'd said, fear in her eyes. "He fell."

I'd found Gideon sprawled on the floor beside the sofa, passed out.

"Daddy's so tired he can't keep his eyes open." My lie left a bitter taste on my tongue.

I'd hustled the children into the bathtub and then off to bed.

This morning, Sharon Rose hadn't seemed to remember the incident. And of course, Gideon couldn't remember it.

But *I* remembered. Bitterly, I remembered.

When will their innocence end, Lord? When will reality settle into my children's tender hearts? When will they look at their father and see . . . and see what I see?

Tears dropped from my eyes into the rich, dark soil of the garden. I dug my glove-covered fingers into the tear-moistened dirt and squeezed.

O God . . . what am I to do?

The crunch of gravel beneath tires drew my gaze to the drive. I recognized Pastor Clyde's new black-and-gray Ford Thunderbird. I yanked off my gloves and wiped the traces of tears from my eyes with the back of my hands; then I stood.

By that time, both doors of the automobile had opened. From the driver's side emerged Pastor Clyde. From the passenger's side came Ken Gordon first, then, from the backseat, Olin Sutherland. Ken and Olin were two of the elders at Amethyst Community Church.

My heart booming, I moved toward them, a welcoming smile pasted on my lips. I tried to speak a greeting but found I couldn't.

"Afternoon, Deborah." Pastor Clyde's tone was calming, like a shepherd's should be. "Is Gideon around? We'd like to speak with him."

"Yes, he's—" I broke off, suddenly not sure where Gideon was and not wanting these men to know that. I felt the heat of embarrassment stain my cheeks.

"Ah, there he is." Pastor Clyde pointed toward the garage.

I turned and saw Gideon bending over the engine of the

Nash. Hadn't he heard our guests arrive, or was he intentionally ignoring their presence?

The pastor's hand alighted on my shoulder, and he gave it a gentle squeeze. I swallowed a lump in my throat.

Three abreast, the men walked toward Gideon while I remained standing by the pastor's automobile.

They knew. They all knew. Why did I try so hard to hide the truth of what was happening in my family?

I swallowed hard a second time, fighting tears of despair as I glanced toward the fenced yard. The children still raced in and out of the spraying water, giggling, shouting, oblivious to all else but the fun they were having. Should I go to them or should I return to my weeding or—

"It's none of your business."

Gideon's angry voice carried to me across the barnyard, drawing my gaze a second time to the garage. Pastor Clyde extended an arm, a gesture of supplication. Gideon braced his hands on the car's fender and stared at him in stubborn silence.

Scarcely aware I did so, I moved closer.

Gideon looked at me and snapped, "Did you ask them to come here?"

I shook my head.

Pastor Clyde said, "We came because we're concerned, Gideon. We care about you. We're your brothers in Christ. If you don't get help, God alone knows what will happen. You could die, Gideon. Do you realize that? Think of your wife and children."

"You're way off base, Pastor." Gideon stepped back, then slammed down the hood of the Nash. "And we're none of your concern."

"Tell me this," Pastor Clyde persisted. "Would you bring

another woman into your home and carry on an affair with her in front of your family?"

"What are you saying? Of course not."

"But you're having an affair with your liquor in front of them. You're choosing the bottle over Deborah and Sharon Rose and Peter, no matter how much it hurts them and yourself. Alcohol has become your mistress."

My husband's face paled, and I gasped softly.

Pastor Clyde continued, his voice low yet strong, "I'm sure you remember the Old Testament story of Jonah. When Jonah ran from obeying God's will, his disobedience caused a storm to arise that threatened to swamp the ship he was on. His disobedience put all the sailors in peril. Don't you see, Gideon? Your disobedience is putting your innocent family's lives in peril, just as Jonah endangered the innocent sailors with him."

Olin Sutherland held out a book. "We think you might find some help in this."

"What is it?" Gideon asked suspiciously.

"It's the manual used in Alcoholics Anonymous."

For a breathless moment, I thought Gideon might go for the elder's throat. Then he turned and strode toward the house, breezing past me without so much as a glance.

I felt surprisingly cold on this warm summer day, and there was an odd humming in my ears.

"Deborah?"

I lifted my gaze to find Pastor Clyde standing right in front of me. He held out the book Olin Sutherland had attempted to give to Gideon. "You should read this."

Why? I wondered as I took it from him. *I'm not the alcoholic.*

"Perhaps you'll gain some understanding."

I understand plenty. I understand the world revolves around Gideon.

I understand the mood of each day depends upon Gideon's mood. I understand everything in our lives hinges upon when he starts to drink and how much he drinks. I understand my needs don't matter. It's all about him, him, him.

"Have you thought about attending some Al-Anon meetings?" Olin asked.

"What's that?"

"It's an organization for those who love an alcoholic."

I looked toward the house. *I'm not sure I do love an alcoholic. Not anymore. I don't know what I feel for sure, but I don't think it's love.*

"Deborah," Pastor Clyde said, "God doesn't mean for us to go through the storms of life alone. We're here to help you, too."

But what could these men do for me? What could anyone do for me as long as Gideon continued to drink?

── *Janelle Burns* ──

It's painful to watch the suffering of a beloved friend, the way I watched Deborah.

She reminded me of a rubber ball, bouncing high, falling low, bouncing back again. One day she was faith filled, hopeful, praying for Gideon for all she was worth. The next she was in despair, looking to God, yet not expecting His answers, not even wanting to pray for Gideon because of her anger. She chose to surrender with one hand and sought to control with the other.

I saw what she was doing, but I wasn't sure she saw it for herself. Confusion is part of alcoholism, not only for those who drink but for their closest family members. I experienced that with my brother, and I recognized what was happening with Deborah as chaos and bewilderment entangled my friend in vicious tentacles.

My husband, Ted, and I prayed for the Clermont family daily. We prayed for Gideon to be delivered. We prayed for Deborah to find peace by trusting completely in the Father. We prayed for safety—physical, mental, and emotional—for the children who were living in a less than ideal situation. We asked that the season of trial might be shortened for the Clermonts, but above all, we prayed that the Lord's will would be done and that He would be glorified in it.

CHAPTER FORTY-ONE

Our marriage was held together by a fragile thread—a thread made from my shaky faith, from my fear of the future, and from my desire that our children not grow up without a father.

But what sort of father do they have?

I remembered that I'd once loved Gideon. I remembered those first months of our marriage. But now those feelings seemed to have belonged to someone else, as if I'd heard about them rather than experienced them firsthand. There were days, moments, when I glimpsed the man Gideon had been, when he could make me laugh or at least smile, when he thought of someone other than himself, when I thought there might be a shred of hope for us.

But those days, those moments, were too few.

Ephesians says a wife must respect her husband. But how could I respect the man I lived with, a man who had no self-control, no self-respect, not even enough backbone to try to change? Gideon seemed more of a child than his son, and Peter was only three years old.

I didn't understand yet that God hadn't said I needed *reasons* to respect my husband. He simply said I *should* respect him. I was commanded to.

If I *had* understood that truth, I would have argued with God about it for it didn't seem just or fair. And I wanted justice. I'd forgotten it was mercy I'd received, time and again, from the Lord.

I didn't pray for Gideon the morning after Pastor Clyde and the two elders came to see us. I was too angry, and I felt guilty for my anger and that guilt only served to make me angrier. If Gideon had listened to what those men had to say . . . if he had accepted that book from Olin Sutherland . . . if he would just try to stop drinking . . .

Gideon was at his surliest when he left the house that morning, skipping breakfast. Richard Johnson was returning today to help rake and bale the hay, and there was Gideon with a monster hangover.

I hope it throbs all day long. I hope your head explodes. I hope you're as miserable as I am.

Oh, what a model Christian wife I was.

When the children had eaten their scrambled eggs and bacon, I dressed them in cotton shorts and shirts, then set them at the kitchen table with crayons and coloring books while I washed the dishes.

A breeze drifted through the open window above the sink. It kissed my wet hands and arms as I moved the plates from the wash water to the rinse water to the drain board. Another time

I might have paused to thank God for the beauty of this morning. Another time I might have let myself enjoy the cool sensations, knowing the heat of a summer day was to follow all too soon.

Another time, but not today.

"Good morning, Gideon!" a man's voice said.

I leaned over the sink, closer to the window, and saw Richard crossing the barnyard to join Gideon beside the old tractor.

I remembered when Andy had bought the faded green John Deere, already an antique, at a farm auction in Middleton. "It'll see us through a couple of seasons," he'd said at the time. "Then we can buy a new one."

All these years later, there it was, the same old tractor. The Clermonts couldn't afford a new one. We never seemed to get ahead enough . . . because of Gideon.

Alfalfa hay promised to bring a good price this year, and it appeared we would have a bumper crop. If we found the right buyer and I managed to keep most of the money tucked away where Gideon couldn't find it and drink it away, perhaps—

"Mommy, can we play in the spwinker again?" Peter asked.

"May we play," I corrected. Then, "Yes, this afternoon you may play in the sprinkler while I work in the garden."

"Goody!"

God, don't let Gideon waste all the money we get from this crop. That's all I'm asking now.

At lunchtime, the men came in from the fields, hungry as well as dusty and sweaty. Richard greeted me warmly as he entered the kitchen, like an old friend.

A quick glance at Gideon, and I could tell he'd had a pick-me-up or two at some time during the morning.

All these years and I could honestly say I'd never smelled liquor on his breath. You would think I could, living with it as I did, but I couldn't. But sometimes I could smell it through the pores of his skin, and always I could see it in his eyes.

When will it end, God? I want it to end!

Fear and anger churned in my belly, and I wondered if I would be sick.

I served the men their lunch—the children and I had already eaten—then I hurried upstairs, wanting to get away from Gideon, wanting to escape the ugly feelings that engulfed me, afraid of what I might do or say if I stayed near him a moment longer.

What happened to the serenity I'd found three weeks ago? What happened to my determination to pray for my husband with new and selfless resolve? Both had vanished like a vapor in the wind.

I glanced into the children's bedroom. They napped atop the covers on their beds. A fan stirred the air, the hum a comforting sound. Sharon Rose slept on her back, an arm over her eyes and her mouth slightly parted. Peter slept on his tummy, his bottom stuck up in the air, knees curled beneath him.

I turned away and entered my room. Suddenly and unexpectedly, the weight of the world seemed to land upon my shoulders. I crumpled, falling to my knees beside the bed. I pressed my forehead against my folded hands—no, they were clenched—and cried out to the Lord.

"I can't take it anymore. O God, I can't. I can't. I can't. Make it stop! I haven't the strength. I haven't the faith. Help me, Jesus."

A broken and repentant heart I will not despise.

"I'm broken, Father. I'm beaten." I struck the bed with my hands. "I never should have married Gideon, should I? But I wasn't following You, Lord. I wasn't listening to You. I rushed into marriage to Gideon. I was running away after Andy died. I was looking for safety, for someone to comfort and take care of me. I should have looked to You, but I didn't. And look what's happened to me because of it."

Do you think I was surprised by what you did, beloved?

I grew still at the thought. *Did* I think God was surprised by what I'd done? Had He known I would make the choices I made? Of course He did. God knew everything.

My works were finished from the foundation of the world, My daughter.

"I don't understand, Father. I don't understand any of this. Why must this happen to me? Why must this happen to us? O God, I don't understand."

— *Richard Johnson* —

I should have seen it coming.

I suspected Gideon had started drinking before the morning was half over. He was good, I'll give him that. I can't recall any time he was out of my sight while we worked, and I sure never caught him taking a swig.

Alcoholics are a crafty lot, but it's a craftiness born of fear, fear that when our body craves alcohol, as it most surely will, a bottle won't be there. In my drinking days, I stashed bottles in toilet tanks and behind Sheetrock between the studs in the walls and beneath floorboards in the closet and between the springs under the seat of my car. I hid bottles more places than I'll live long enough to remember.

Yeah, we're crafty, but as booze ravages our brains, as the blackouts become more frequent, we forget where we stashed things, which makes it even more important to have those bottles hidden everywhere.

Thank God—and only by His grace—He delivered me from my addiction. I was praying for the same miracle for Gideon Clermont.

Over lunch, after Deborah left the kitchen, I tried talking to him. I told him I used to be a drinking man and how God saved me. "If He hadn't," I told him, "I'd be dead."

Man, I saw the fear in Gideon's eyes. He knew he was killing himself. And he knew he was killing his marriage, too, driving away the wife he loved. He could fight the truth all he wanted, but he knew it.

"Sobriety's only the first step," I told him. "We've got to believe God can restore us to a better way of living and thinking. We ask Him to give us the strength to change. We ask Him for the wisdom to know how and what to change."

You know the old saying: You can lead a horse to water but you can't make it drink. Well, that's how recovery is for the alcoholic. He's got to want it. Really want it. Want it more than he wants his booze.

Gideon wasn't there yet.

CHAPTER FORTY-TWO

A broken and repentant heart I will not despise. . . . Do you think I was surprised by what you did, beloved . . . ? My works were finished from the foundation of the world, My daughter.

By rote I worked in my garden, weeding and hoeing, while my mind replayed those words over and over and over again. I tried to make sense of them. I *wanted* to make sense of them.

I wanted my life to make sense.

I wanted my marriage to make sense.

I wanted to do and be what God wanted me to do and be.

I was failing.

Miserably failing.

I heard the rumble of the tractor as it returned to the barnyard. I didn't look up. I hadn't the heart to look up. I heard the grating sound the tractor always made when Gideon shifted into reverse.

Heidi began to bark.

"Daddy! Daddy!" Peter's excited voice reached my ears.

A voice not coming from the backyard. I straightened, twisted, stared horrified as Peter ran toward the rear of the tractor.

"Gideon!" I screamed. "Peter!" I jumped to my feet. "Gideon!"

He didn't hear me. Or couldn't hear me. And he wasn't looking behind him as he backed the tractor toward the place he always parked it. Too fast. He was backing up too fast.

I waved my arms, even though he wasn't looking my way, and shouted, "Gideon, stop!" By now, I was running too.

Peter's chubby little legs were surprisingly fast, but they wouldn't be fast enough to move out of the path of the tractor. *God, help!*

The next few seconds played out almost like a slow-motion scene at the movies. Peter tripped—perhaps over a rut in the ground, perhaps over his own feet—and pitched forward, tumbling beyond the reach of the large John Deere tire. Seconds later—seconds that seemed an eternity—the tractor came to a halt and the engine died.

All sense of slow motion vanished. Everything happened quickly now.

Peter began to cry just as I grabbed him from the ground. His knees were scraped and so was his left cheek and chin, but otherwise, he seemed okay. I hugged him tightly to me as I whirled toward the tractor.

Twisting on the seat, his hands still on the steering wheel, Gideon stared at us, a confused look on his face.

"You could have killed your son!" I screamed at him in icy rage. "You almost killed Peter!"

"I . . . I didn't see him. I didn't know he was behind me."

"You weren't even looking. You weren't looking because you weren't thinking. And we both know why you weren't. You're drunk. I can see it in your eyes." I whirled toward the backyard. "Sharon Rose, can you get my purse from upstairs? Mommy needs to go into town." Then, with icy calm, I glanced over my shoulder and said, "I want you to go away, Gideon. I want you to go far away and leave us in peace. I want you to leave while we're in town."

"Leave? Deb, he just took a little spill. Peter's not really hurt."

"Not this time. But what about next time? I can't risk the next time, Gideon. I want you to go. I want you to go and leave us alone."

Perhaps sensing my mood more than understanding my words, Peter started to sob. I cupped the back of his head with my hand and carried him into the house, where I quickly washed his face and knees and applied a couple of Band-Aids to the scrapes.

A short while later, Sharon Rose and Peter sat beside me on the front seat and Heidi lay on the backseat as I pulled out of the garage, careful not to look toward the tractor, not wanting to catch even a glimpse of Gideon.

"Where are we going, Mommy?" Sharon Rose asked.

"For ice cream." I feigned a smile. "Mommy just wanted some ice cream, and I thought you'd want some, too."

The ploy worked. Sharon Rose and Peter both brightened, seeming to forget their parents' fight and Peter's scrapes. They couldn't know my heart had turned to stone and lay cold and heavy in my chest.

I drove to Julia's Café and parked the car on the street. I let Heidi out and told her to lie down in the shade under the awning, which she obediently did. "Stay," I commanded. Then

Sharon Rose, Peter, and I went inside the restaurant. Except for us, it was empty of customers.

"Well, look who's come to see us." Alice Gordon grinned broadly at the children. "What brings you here?"

"Ice cream," my daughter and son chorused.

Sharon Rose added, "I want chocolate."

Peter said, "I want 'nilla."

"Mmm. Ice cream. Best thing for a hot summer day." Alice winked at me. "What about you, Deborah? You want chocolate and 'nilla, too?"

A quick look at the menu, and we decided to share a triple-decker sundae with all the fixings. The children thought it was great fun to rise up on their knees, lean over the banana-shaped bowl, and dig their spoons into the sweet, gooey mess. Soon their faces and fingers were stained with chocolate, strawberries, and whipped cream.

I laughed with them when they laughed, but there wasn't any joy in me. In truth, it felt as if my face would crack from the effort to smile. I hurt inside, a keening kind of hurt.

Somehow I kept my mask firmly in place as I cleaned the children's faces and hands with the damp cloth Alice brought me. I kept it in place as I bid her and Luke Lopez, the owner, a good day. I kept it in place throughout the drive home, my eyes fixed on the road straight ahead, my hands gripping the wheel like a vise.

I don't know what I hoped or expected to find at home. Would Gideon be gone or would he still be there? Would he comply with my request or would he argue with me? What would I do if he refused to leave? What would I do if he left and never came back? I knew what I'd told him I wanted, but what did I really want?

And what does God want?

He must want Gideon to leave, I reasoned. God wouldn't want my children put into danger. Gideon had to leave. He had to.

I slowed the Nash as our property neared, clicked on my left signal, then turned into the drive. Merle Johnson's pickup truck was parked near the back porch . . . and seated on the porch were Gideon and Richard.

I started to cry.

Gertrude Johnson

I asked Merle where on earth his nephew was going with our pickup, and all that man would say to me was, "I didn't ask. Ain't none of my business, Gertie."

Well, I ask you, why in heaven's name wasn't it his business? It was our truck.

Still, when I got a look at the grim expression on Richard's face, I didn't have the courage to ask either. But I did watch out the window when he left, and I did see that he drove straight over to the Clermont place. Short while later, I was still watching when I saw the Clermonts' car turning into their drive.

I had a feeling that whatever was afoot wasn't good. What's the word for that? Oh, I know. A premonition. That's what I had. A premonition.

CHAPTER FORTY-THREE

I managed to hide my tears from Sharon Rose and Peter. With steely resolve I brought my emotions under control, opened the car doors to let the children and dog out, and then we all headed toward the house.

"We had ice cream, Daddy," Sharon Rose called.

I couldn't quite describe the look Gideon gave his daughter. More than painful. Beyond desperate.

"Hey, kids," Richard said cheerfully. "How'd you like me to push you on the swing? We'll see how high you can go." He stepped off the porch and motioned toward the backyard. "Is that okay, Deborah?" His gaze, filled with compassion, touched mine for a moment.

"Go ahead," I told the children. "Mommy's going to stay here and talk to Daddy."

Richard took Sharon Rose's right hand and Peter's left hand and walked away, Heidi following right behind them.

It took several moments before I had the courage to turn my gaze toward Gideon. He was standing now, a suitcase near his right leg.

My stomach sank. He was going. It was what I wanted, and yet . . .

Dark half-moons underscored his eyes, giving him a haunted look. His skin had an unhealthy pallor beneath his suntan. I realized then that he'd lost weight in recent weeks. His clothes hung on him, as if they belonged to someone else.

"Deb?"

I barely heard him speak my name.

"Deb, I'm sorry."

"You're sorry. You're always sorry."

"You know I'd never intentionally hurt you. And I'd rather cut off my right arm than have anything happen to one of the kids. I . . . I just . . . " He let the sentence drift off, unfinished.

"You might not mean to hurt us, Gideon, but you do it anyway. Maybe not with a tractor, but in plenty of other ways."

"God forgive me."

God might forgive you, Gideon, but I'm not sure I can . . . I'm not sure I can.

"I'm going to stop drinking, Deb."

Despair gave way to bitterness. "I've heard that promise before." I climbed the steps, brushed past him, and walked to the porch swing. I sat down before the unsteadiness of my legs let me fall.

Gideon turned toward me but he didn't approach. He must have sensed I didn't want him too close. "I mean it this time. I'm going to beat this thing."

This thing.

"I've tried, you know. I've tried to keep my promises to you.

I'd get up in the mornings and I'd swear I wouldn't have a drink. And then something would happen." He swallowed hard, and his Adam's apple bobbed. "Or nothing would happen . . . and the next thing I knew I'd have a drink."

"Or two or three or four."

He stared at me with those haunted, beaten eyes. Why hadn't I noticed that before? When had I stopped looking at him, stopped seeing, really seeing?

"Yes," he whispered. "Or two or three or four."

I glanced at the suitcase. "Where are you going?"

"Richard knows of a place." He hesitated, then said, "A place for alcoholics."

That drew my gaze back to him. Never had he used that word before. He'd danced around it countless times, but never had he said it. But then, had I been much different? The word made me feel ashamed, and I wasn't even the one who drank.

"Deb?"

"What?"

"When I get sober, when I *stay* sober, may I come home?"

The air was hot and dry, and I could scarcely breathe. "I don't know, Gideon. I . . . I just don't know."

Tears welled in his eyes, and he made no attempt to hide them from me or to brush them away as they fell down his cheeks. "I understand," he said, his voice low and scratchy. He reached down and picked up his suitcase. "I . . . I'll send word to you through Richard, and you can do the same if you want." He turned and headed down the steps.

"Gideon!" I jumped to my feet.

He stopped and looked over his shoulder.

My heart hammered. I clasped my hands together; my palms were slick with sweat. "I'll pray for you."

The saddest of smiles curved the corners of his mouth. "Thanks. I'll need all the prayers I can get." The smile vanished as quickly as it had come. "Do you suppose God'll want to hear from me after all I've done?"

Yes. I wanted to say it aloud, but I couldn't get the word out of my throat.

Through a veil of tears, I saw my husband walk to Merle Johnson's pickup, toss his suitcase into the truck bed, then climb into the passenger seat where he waited, motionless, for Richard.

— *Henry Richardson* —

It was almost five years since my son-in-law wound up in the hospital from that fall off the ladder. Who knew, back then, that it would keep getting worse for my girl?

Of course, she always did her best to keep the truth from her mother and me. She put on a brave face, but Bernice and I could tell when she was on that roller coaster.

And if we couldn't, there was still the little ones. You can't keep kids from speaking the truth. They just open their mouths and out it comes. Small things, like how their mommy cried sometimes when she did the dishes, like how sometimes Mommy couldn't wake Daddy up when he fell asleep on the couch.

Two and two always make four.

I knew. Bernice and I both knew, and it tore us up inside. But let us dare say a word that sounded like criticism of Gideon, and Deborah stiffened like a plank. She'd speak up in his defense, even when it was obvious he was the one giving her so much grief.

She should've left him. She should've packed up and left him before that first year was out, before Sharon Rose was born. But she didn't. Heaven knows why.

Well, maybe heaven *does* know why. Deborah put a lot of stock in that Bible of hers. Me, I always believed you couldn't go wrong with the Golden Rule and the Ten Commandments. But my daughter . . . well, it was different for her. She really wanted to *live* what the Bible said, cover to cover.

Can't see that wanting to live it made her life any easier.

CHAPTER FORTY-FOUR

I couldn't sleep the night after Gideon went away. I lay on my bed, tossing, turning, weeping. I was numb and yet I ached at the same time.

"What do I do, Father?" I whispered into that too-silent room. "What do I do now?"

Exhausted and frustrated, I arose. I slipped a cotton robe over my pajamas, put on my sandals, and went outside. When Heidi would have gone with me, I told her to stay on the porch.

The night was absolutely still. No breeze stirred the trees. No crickets chirped. No birds sang.

Silence. Only silence.

I walked into the alfalfa field. Hay bales lay in straight rows over about a quarter of the acreage. Forgotten bales that hadn't been stacked because of what Gideon had done, because Gideon was gone.

I stopped and looked up at the twinkling stars against an inky backdrop.

"What would You have me do?" I screamed the words into the vastness of the night, not expecting an answer.

How could I possibly find words to describe what happened then?

A strange, comforting warmth filled me, starting in the center of my being and moving out to the tips of my extremities, to my fingertips and my toes and the top of my head. Then I heard a voice, silent, yet strangely audible.

I will give you a new heart with new and right desires, and I will put a new spirit in you. I will take out your stony heart of sin and give you a new, obedient heart.

I dropped to my knees, mindless of the hay stubble.

"Take my heart of stone, Lord," I whispered, my head bowed. "Give me a new, obedient one." I drew a shaky breath, then added, "I surrender. Not my will but Thine. Not my will but Thine."

I don't know how long I remained on my knees. Ten minutes? An hour? But eventually I stood and returned to the house. I climbed the stairs, shucked off my robe, lay down on the bed . . . and slept.

Sharon Rose was playing with her dolls and teddy bears in the living room and Peter was building something with his blocks when Richard Johnson came to the house later on that Saturday morning. I saw his approach before he reached the porch, so I met him at the screen door, holding it open for him to enter.

"Would you like some coffee?" I asked.

"Yes, thanks."

I motioned for him to sit at the table, then went to fill two large cups with the dark brew. I took my time as I put them on a tray, along with the sugar bowl and creamer, and carried it to the table. I lifted one cup and set it before Richard. Then I sat across from him, took the other cup, spooned sugar and poured cream into my coffee, and sipped the hot drink. All this I did without once looking at Richard.

But finally, I was ready to meet his gaze. "How is he?"

"He had a rough night." Richard shook his head. "The first few days of withdrawal are the worst. His emotions are pretty raw. He's carrying a load of guilt right now."

My defenses rose up. *Is that my fault? I didn't make him lie. I didn't make him drink. I didn't make him behave so stupidly that he might have killed our son.*

Richard leaned toward me. "Listen, Deborah. I doubt Gideon told you this. He probably didn't have time to tell you, but I'm an alcoholic, too."

My face must have revealed surprise.

"I've been sober for eight years now. God restored me to sanity, and He can do the same thing for Gideon, if he's ready to let Him. I think he is ready. I think he's finally hit bottom and is ready to start climbing out of that hole he's in."

"Gideon's promised so many times that he'll quit. How do I know he'll really do it this time?"

"Promises are easy." He shrugged. "Sobriety isn't. It takes being willing to turn our lives over to God. It takes choosing a whole new way of thinking."

I glanced out the screen door, remembering what had happened to me in the night. Surrender. Giving up my will for His. Living His way instead of my way.

*What do I choose to do, Lord, even though I know it's displeasing
to You? Am I so different from Gideon? What's my sin of choice?*

Richard said, "Gideon wants me to ask if there's hope for
the two of you. He wants to know if there's any chance you'll
be able to love him again."

I didn't fail to notice that Gideon hadn't asked if I *still* loved
him. He'd asked if I *could* love him. He'd already seen the hard-
ness of my heart. Now he wanted to look toward the future.

Hope deferred makes the heart sick. That's what the Bible said. If
I took away the last shred of Gideon's hope, wouldn't that be
displeasing to God?

I looked at Richard, answering softly, "Gideon has to have
hope. Without it, he—" My voice broke and the tears came,
despite my efforts not to let myself cry.

"Hold on to *your* hope, too, Deborah." Richard placed a
hand over mine. "It'll get better. I've seen God do too many
miracles not to believe He'll work them again."

I wanted to believe in a miracle for Gideon and me. I desperately wanted to believe it. I knew God could work miracles. The
question was, would He?

O Father, I believe. Help now my unbelief.

"Mommy," called Sharon Rose from the living room, "I'm
hungry. Can we eat?"

Hastily, I dashed away the tears; then I stood and went to
the sink. "Mommy will fix your lunch right now, Sharon Rose."
I splashed water onto my cheeks and dried my face with the
hand towel. "Richard, would you care to join us?"

"Thanks, but no." The scrape of chair legs on the linoleum
floor told me he'd risen. "I need to give Uncle Merle a hand
with a few things; then I've got to drive back to the center.
I told Gideon I'd see him again this afternoon."

I drew a deep breath. "I never asked where you took him. What sort of place is it?"

"It's called Victory House. It's in the mountains north of Boise. A Christian couple runs it. I met the husband several years ago at a conference. Don't worry. Gideon's getting good care, and over the next month, he'll be learning the tools he needs to overcome his addiction."

"A month?" My eyes widened as I turned around. "What's this going to cost?"

"Don't worry about that now."

Just when *was* I supposed to worry about it, if not now? After we were bankrupt? After we lost our farm, our home? We hadn't any savings. We hadn't any income except for what the sale of the hay crop would bring, and we would need that for other things.

Thanks to Gideon, we'd never had a chance to get ahead. Thanks to Gideon—

O God, how do I turn off these bitter thoughts? How can I leave my worries with You? How do I stop resenting what Gideon has done?

Last night I'd found peace. Ever elusive, it had slipped away again.

How do I hold on to You and Your peace, Lord? Help me hold on to hope.

I'd heard Pastor Clyde teach on offering ourselves as a living and holy sacrifice to God. "The problem with a living sacrifice," he'd said, "is that it's prone to crawling off the altar."

At the time, I'd chuckled along with the rest of the congregation. I didn't find it so amusing now. It was too true to be funny.

"Deborah," Richard said, "extend a little grace to yourself.

God doesn't expect perfection from us. He wants progress but He knows we'll never be perfect. Take it one day at a time."

Bernice Richardson

Have you even the slightest notion what it's like to see your own daughter trapped in a situation like Deborah's? I hope not, for your sake.

Why Gideon didn't pull himself up by his own bootstraps long before, I would never understand.

I was beside myself when Deborah called to tell us what was going on. Gideon was staying in some sort of clinic or sanitarium or some such, and Deborah and the children were out at that farm alone.

Oh, there was more happening than she let on. I was no fool.

I wanted my daughter happy, and I didn't see how she ever would be, married to a . . . a . . . Well, you know. Gideon had a d-r-i-n-k-i-n-g problem.

"We're fine, Mother," she kept saying.

Well, I could hear the pain behind those words. She wasn't fine. She wasn't fine at all. What that poor girl had to suffer . . . it was too much. It was simply too much.

I tried to convince her to pack her bags and come stay with her father and me, but she wouldn't do it. She was as stubborn as she'd ever been. She wouldn't move home after Andy's death, and she wouldn't move home now, either.

"This is different," I told her. "You didn't have children before."

Do you know what she said to that? She said, "All the more reason to stay." Now, does that make sense to you?

"You're already living alone," I said the last time we spoke. "You might as well get a divorce and be legally free. Divorce isn't considered as shameful as it used to be. Don't you *want* to be happy?"

I'll never forget the tone of her voice—soft and yearning—when she answered, "Mother, I want whatever God wants for me."

I was raised in a Christian home and have been a steady churchgoer all my life, but I can't say I understand my daughter's stubborn faith. I don't understand it at all.

CHAPTER FORTY-FIVE

"Soviet ballet dancer Rudolf Nureyev defected to the West last Friday while his troupe was in Paris. In a statement released—"

I clicked off the radio, disinterested in what happened in the world beyond my own small borders.

Silence engulfed me. An unnatural silence for a house used to the sounds of little children. After several phone calls from my mother over the six days since Gideon's departure, I'd finally relented and allowed Sharon Rose and Peter to go visit their grandparents.

In truth, I'd thought it would make things easier if I didn't constantly have to hide my emotions from them. Now I wasn't so sure it was a wise decision. The days seemed too long, too empty. Too much time to think. I would have welcomed some distraction.

I went out to the porch, where I leaned my shoulder against

one of the posts. The day was mild and soft. A gentle but steady breeze pushed powder-puff clouds across the sky.

My gaze fell on the stacked bales of hay against the side of the barn. They were all there now. Several men from Amethyst Community Church had shown up on Monday and brought in all the bales that had been left in the field. Later, others had dropped by to help with the irrigating and to mow the backyard.

I had the feeling no one from my church—except Pastor Clyde and his wife, whom I'd personally told—knew what had happened to Gideon. Nor did anyone ask. They were simply there, my neighbors, my Christian brethren, offering to share the load. Not judging, just loving.

I took a deep breath, and as I let it out, I thanked God for the body of Christ.

Heidi appeared around the corner of the house and trotted toward me, her tongue hanging out one side of her mouth.

"You miss Sharon Rose and Peter, too, don't you, girl?" I sat on the top step and waited for the collie to reach me. Then I stroked her head, gently ruffling her ears. "They'll be home on Saturday."

I shifted my position, leaning my back against the wooden railing. I drew one knee to my chest and hugged it to me with my arms.

"I miss Gideon," I whispered.

With a little groan as commentary, Heidi lay down next to me.

I stroked the dog's head. "But do I miss him only because I'm used to him being around? Will I be able to love him as a wife should love her husband? Would I be more content if he never came home?"

"For I hate divorce!" says the Lord, the God of Israel.

Those words had come to me as a promise; then they'd seemed like a death sentence, a curse. Could they become a promise again?

Hold on to hope. That's what Richard Johnson had told me. *I'm trying. Dear God, I'm trying.*

I'd stayed awake late into the night, reading the book Olin Sutherland had given me the week before. There were times I felt as if the writers of that book had been looking right into my home, right into my own marriage . . . right into my heart.

Perhaps that was what gave me a small measure of comfort today. Knowing I wasn't the only woman who'd found herself in these circumstances and behaved in the ways I'd behaved.

I frowned, bothered by my thoughts. Was normal behavior necessarily right behavior?

Whenever trouble comes your way, let it be an opportunity for joy.

I closed my eyes and pressed the heels of my hands against my ears. How often would God bring that same passage of Scripture to my mind? He had taken me to the book of James many times through the years—after Andy died, when I was in danger of losing Sharon Rose, and now this, now with Gideon.

Whenever trouble comes your way, let it be an opportunity for joy.

Perhaps God would keep reminding me of these verses until I counted my troubles joy.

For when your faith is tested, your endurance has a chance to grow. So let it grow, for when your endurance is fully developed, you will be strong in character and ready for anything.

Surrender.

I opened my eyes and stared up at the heavens. "I *try* to surrender, God," I shouted. "I *want* to surrender, but I don't know *how!*"

Startled by my outburst, Heidi sat up and nudged me with

her nose. I grabbed her around the neck and buried my face in her rough fur. I was tired. So tired. Tired of striving. Tired of dreading the unknown future.

Worship Me, beloved.

I grew still.

Trust Me, beloved.

I held my breath.

No matter what happens, always be thankful, for this is God's will for you who belong to Christ Jesus.

"Be thankful," I whispered, feeling the words as much as speaking them. "Be thankful no matter what happens, for that is God's will for me."

Understanding swept over me. God was telling me how to surrender. I was to be thankful and worship Him, no matter what happened in my life. No matter what happened with Gideon. No matter if things were easy or hard.

No matter what, worship the Lord.

— *Richard Johnson* —

Deborah was different when next I saw her. She asked about Gideon, and I could tell she wasn't asking because it was expected of her. She wanted to know because she cared.

As glad as I was to see this change, I didn't try to soften my answers. I told her things don't get easier in recovery right away, and she couldn't expect too much too soon. She had to fight the desire to second-guess and the need to control the situation.

The worst part of the withdrawal process was behind Gideon, I told her, but the hard work had just begun. Gideon had to change his whole way of thinking if he wanted to maintain long-term sobriety. That was the goal. To never take another drink. He had to look to God to change him from the inside out.

Getting rid of the garbage, facing our faults and the wrongs we've done to others, is grueling work. Ask anyone who's been through it. They'll tell you.

I've seen God work miracles in the past few years. I've seen Him change the helpless and hopeless into productive members of society. Occasionally, God removes the desire to drink from a man's heart and mind with the precision of a surgeon cutting out a cancer. But most often, He yokes Himself to His child and walks him through, one step at a time, one day at a time.

That was what He was doing with Gideon.

CHAPTER FORTY-SIX

The month Gideon was away seemed to last forever. Yet at the same time, when the end came, it didn't seem long enough.

Gideon's coming home today.

My stomach fluttered at the thought. Nerves? Fear? Dread? Anticipation?

All that and more.

With the exception of two phone calls made in his final week at Victory House, there had been no communication between us. Those two conversations had been brief and awkward. He'd told me how sorry he was, and he'd promised I would find him a new man if I decided to give him another chance.

A new man.

What did that mean? Had I ever known who Gideon's "old man" was? Who would this new man be? I couldn't be sure. I couldn't be sure of anything about my husband of five and a half years.

How terribly sad that was.

We're starting over, Father. Teach me how to show Gideon my respect. It won't be easy, Lord, because I don't . . . I don't feel it yet. How can I, when he's done all he could to destroy it?

I stared at my reflection in the mirror on my bedroom wall. Last week, I'd walked into the Curly Q Hair and Nail Salon and told Elaine, the beautician, to cut my hair off. Pixie short. Shorter than I'd worn it in my life. I wondered if Gideon would like it. I did. Would he?

Do I care if he likes it? I wondered, wanting to care but not sure I did.

The outfit I wore was new, too. Our financial circumstances being as they were, I shouldn't have spent the money, but I'd done it anyway. I'd *needed* to look pretty. The cotton slacks were robin's-egg blue, and the sleeveless top was blue-and-white checked. The pale colors showed off my suntan and made my eyes seem bluer.

Will Gideon find me attractive?

He'd shown little husbandly attention to me for so long. Months and months. I'd often wondered if the fault was my own, if I was undesirable. When was the last time he'd tried to hold my hand or stroke my hair?

Forever. It seems like forever.

I drew a deep breath as I turned from the mirror. I left the bedroom and went downstairs.

The house was quiet. I'd sent the children to my parents' home for the night. Although I knew Gideon would be anxious to see Sharon Rose and Peter, I also knew we needed some time together, just the two of us, husband and wife.

"Will we make it, God? Can we overcome the past? How will I believe him when he makes promises? How can I be sure this time is different, that he really has stopped for good?"

In the weeks Gideon was away, I'd educated myself. I'd read the book from Alcoholics Anonymous and every other piece of literature I could find on the topic. For the first time, I'd begun to grasp the reality before me, before us. I'd acknowledged the part I'd played, had begun to see the mistakes I'd made, had realized my futile efforts to control both Gideon and the alcoholism itself.

I was scared.

I was hopeful.

I was terrified.

I was confident.

Whenever trouble comes your way, let it be an opportunity for joy.

This was one of my opportunities for joy.

Seconds before I heard the crunch of gravel on the driveway, Heidi went to the back door, ears alert as she stared through the screen door.

He's here.

I gulped in another breath, staving off a wave of panic. My mouth was dry as dust. My stomach was tied in a dozen knots. What if—

If God is for me, who can be against me?

I joined Heidi at the doorway. Merle Johnson's pickup truck rolled to a stop, and moments later, the engine died. Sunlight glinted off the front windshield, obscuring the occupants from view.

O God, be with us.

I opened the screen and went outside, stopping at the top of the porch steps. Seconds stretched into hours while I waited for the passenger door to open.

I swallowed hard.

Gideon got out of the cab, suitcase in hand. He was wearing jeans and a gray plaid shirt tucked into the waistband. His hair was neatly trimmed. He looked . . . different.

I descended the steps and stopped again.

With a measured pace, he approached me, and I realized he was every bit as nervous as I was. Still, his gaze didn't waver from mine. A steady vision. A clear vision.

Oh, Gideon, Gideon. I want it to work out. I do. If only . . .

He stopped before he reached me. "Hi, Deb."

"Gideon."

"You look great." He smiled, and I caught a glimpse of the Gideon I'd first met. "You cut your hair. I like it."

I touched my nape with the fingers of my right hand. "Thanks." I smiled a little too. "I . . . I'm glad you like it. I was afraid you wouldn't."

He glanced past me, toward the back porch.

"The children are with my parents."

"Oh."

"I thought we should have time to talk."

He looked at me again. "Sure. I understand."

The truck started again. Gideon turned and waved, then watched as Richard backed the pickup down the drive.

"Gideon?"

"Yeah?"

"I'm scared."

He met my gaze again. "Me, too."

"Do you think we'll be okay?"

"I hope so, Deb," he answered softly. "I'll give it everything I've got."

My heart thudded erratically. My pulse thrummed in my

ears. I felt as if I were standing on the edge of a cliff above a cold mountain lake and all the spectators were waiting to see if I would throw myself out, away from the rocks, and dive into the water below.

And so I jumped.

"Me, too, Gideon," I whispered. "Me, too."

— *Gideon Clermont* —

No one sets out to become an alcoholic. Least of all me.

Sure, I did my share of drinking with buddies in the army. Everybody did. Men—*real* men—are supposed to be able to hold their liquor. You can't *not* drink when everybody else is. At least, that's what the devil whispers in your ear.

When I met Andy Haskins in Korea, things changed for me. He led me to faith in Jesus Christ. I guess the problem was, I was ready for a Savior, but I never let Him be Lord. And I failed to understand a believer's need for the body of Christ. There's a reason the Bible tells us not to forsake gathering together with other believers. Because without them, we suffer. When you see a Christian neglecting being in fellowship, you're seeing a Christian in spiritual trouble. But I'm getting ahead of myself.

Those months after I accepted Christ into my heart, I walked close to Him. Of course, I had Andy as a mentor. He took me on a journey into the written Word, and I loved it. But after I got out of the military and went home to California, things changed for me. I hung out with my old friends. I couldn't find a church I liked. I couldn't find a job.

That's what finally brought me to Idaho. I came here to work for Andy, only Andy was dead. I arrived the day of the funeral. His death hit me hard, harder than I'd expected it to.

And then there was Deb. Truth is, I started to fall in love the moment I laid eyes on her. I'd known she was special because Andy talked about her all the time in Korea, but seeing her for the first time . . . she took my breath away, even in her black dress, hat, and veil.

I never meant to put her through what I did. I wouldn't wish that on my worst enemy, let alone Deb. Yet it's the woman I profess to love who suffered the most. You always hurt the ones you love. Isn't that how the saying goes? That was sure true for me.

When did my social drinking change to an obsession? It's hard to pinpoint, really. It was so subtle, I didn't recognize the starting point of my spiral into hell. I guess it began when I started drinking to escape. When things didn't go my way. When I had a bad day or a fight with my wife. When I was stressed or in emotional pain. That's when I drank. Hey, who wouldn't? Right?

Oh, man. How easy it is to justify our sins.

I hid my drinking from Deb, especially as it increased, as it became a compulsion. I knew she didn't like it when I consumed alcohol. The pattern of deception had already begun.

The next thing I knew, I didn't need stress or a problem for a reason to drink. I'd get up after Deb went to sleep and I'd gulp down a drink or two. Maybe three. But I could handle three. I never felt a buzz. Never did anything stupid. I could still control when I started drinking. Or so I thought. Denial with a capital *D*.

Was God trying to talk to me during this time? You bet. Funny thing is, I thought I could hide it from Him the same way I was hiding it from my wife. I thought if I ignored those gentle tugs on my heart, He wouldn't notice what I was doing.

About the time Deb got pregnant with Sharon Rose, something changed radically within me. I started drinking earlier and earlier in the day, and I had trouble stopping. I thought I was fooling everybody. I know I was fooling Deb. She was so trusting, so naive. Then she almost lost the baby, and I lost my job because I was drunk at work.

Most folks would wonder why that wasn't enough to make me stop. It's hard to answer that question except to say the fire of my addiction was burning white hot in my belly by that time.

It would have served me right if I'd lost my wife while I was in the hospital, if she'd moved back to the farm without me, if she'd never let me see my daughter. Only God knows why Deb hung in there with me. I'll never understand it. Not even if I live a thousand years.

By the time we were living on the farm, I'd grown dependent on Deb. I was full of fear and anxiety. My confidence disappeared. I was grateful when Deb made decisions so I didn't have to. Decisions about finances and crops and raising our kids and when to go to church and all the small details that make up a life. A lot of it passed in a haze for me anyway.

Oh, I'd have periods of sobriety. Deb would catch me in a lie or with a bottle again, and I'd swear I wouldn't do it anymore. But those dry spells didn't last. The pull, the desire, the temptation soon won out, and each of those periods of drinking that followed would be worse and last longer than the one before.

I knew by then that I was a liar and a cheat. I was the scum of the earth. I knew I was a drunkard. I knew it, but I couldn't admit it. Not to myself. Certainly not to anybody else. Pride was the reason. Some say pride is at the root of all sin. I think maybe they're right.

For quite a while, I was able to maintain a fairly normal life. Turns out, I was a pretty good farmer in addition to being a skilled carpenter, and I supported my wife and kids. Well, most of the time I did.

I hated it when Deb watched me so closely. I was ingenious when it came to hiding my bottles, but every so often, I fouled up. I brushed my teeth frequently so she wouldn't smell booze on my breath. I was crafty, cunning, manipulative. I was a mess.

"If you love me," Deb would say when I was at my worst, "why won't you stop? Why are you doing this to us?"

I had no answer. I didn't understand it myself. I didn't *want* to live the way I was living.

"God will help you if you ask Him," she would say.

That always made me angry. I knew it was true. She didn't have to keep reminding me. Hey, sometimes I'd sit with an open Bible on my lap and ask God to deliver me . . . then I'd lift that bottle and take another drink without blinking an eye.

Self-will run amok.

But God *did* deliver me. Not because I deserved it, mind you, but because of His grace and mercy alone. He sent Richard at just the right time to show me a way out. He put me in a place where I could face the truth about myself.

Not just face it. Admit it and confess it, to Him and to others.

I'm an alcoholic.

I'm sober now. I'm working the steps of Alcoholics Anonymous. I'm depending on God because I've learned I can't do it without Him. I'm making amends, to the best of my ability, to those I've injured.

I know it won't be easy. I guess I'll always be an alcoholic, same as I'll always be a sinner. But I'm a sinner saved by grace, and by His grace I can choose to be a sober alcoholic.

I realized that making Jesus my Savior isn't enough. He has to be Lord of my life, too. So every morning now, I ask Him to sit on the throne of my heart and to rule there throughout my day . . . throughout my life.

I pray to God that Deb will want to walk through that life with me.

PART FIVE

1964

What is faith?

It is the confident assurance that

what we hope for is going to happen.

It is the evidence of things we cannot yet see.

HEBREWS 11:1

EPILOGUE

My love for Gideon returned quickly.

My trust came more slowly.

I was often afraid in the first year of Gideon's recovery. Little things he did triggered the fear response. I had to reject that response one day at a time, the same way Gideon had to choose sobriety one day at a time. Together we learned new ways of communicating. Together we sought God's help. Together we surrendered our will for His. Together we found happiness and contentment.

It was on the second anniversary of Gideon's recovery that I realized I believed—*really* believed—he was going to make it. In a sudden moment of clarity, I believed that he was truly determined not to take another drink and that he wasn't acting for my benefit. I saw that the changes in him had deep roots and wouldn't be easily ripped up.

Oh, I understand the reality of alcoholism. It's cunning and baffling, and the enemy prowls about, seeking to destroy. But I also understand our God is a big God, a God of second chances, a God of renewal, a God of miracles.

I used to wonder why my life took the direction it did. What would have happened if I hadn't married Gideon? After all, I married in haste. I wasn't seeking God's wisdom, didn't ask the Lord if I should marry again. For a time, I even wondered if living with an alcoholic was my punishment for rebellion, the bed I'd made and had to lie in.

But now I believe this was all by God's design. I believe God put us together as man and wife so we could drive each other to the foot of the cross. Where we belonged.

You see, God uses everything for good in our lives when we love Him and are called according to His purpose for us. He uses everything. Even Gideon's alcoholism.

Not so very long ago, my life was filled with shadows. I feared what tomorrow would bring. I was a woman without hope. But praise God, I've learned there is hope beyond the shadows.

You will have courage because you will have hope.

You will be protected and will rest in safety. You will lie down

unafraid, and many will look to you for help.

JOB 11:18-19

A NOTE FROM THE AUTHOR

Dear Friends:

When God first began placing this story on my heart, I knew it wouldn't be an easy one to write. The alcoholism of a loved one has touched me and my family, so Deborah's story, although fictional, was also personal. I have known fear and denial and rage and shame and guilt and grief. I have been that person at the end of both her rope and her hope. But I have also found that when I am at the end of myself, that's where I find Jesus, cradling me in His arms, restoring my hope. He is faithful even when I am faithless.

In his book *The Purpose Driven Life*, Rick Warren writes, "God *never wastes a hurt!* In fact, your *greatest* ministry will most likely come out of your greatest hurt. . . . God intentionally allows you to go through painful experiences to equip you for ministry to others."

I read that paragraph not long after I finished writing *Beyond the Shadows*, and my heart quickened as I remembered the verses God gave me to end this novel: *"You will have courage because you will have hope. You will be protected and will rest in safety. You will lie down unafraid, and many will look to you for help"* (Job 11:18-19).

God hasn't wasted the hurt of alcoholism in my life. He used it to teach me about the importance of surrendering my all to Him. He used it to equip me for ministry to others. He used it to help me write this novel. He took me inside my deepest hurts and fears, and I discovered courage because of my hope in Him.

Beloved, there is hope beyond the shadows in your life. His name is Jesus.

In the grip of His grace,

Robin Lee Hatcher

From her heart . . . to yours.
www.robinleehatcher.com
robinlee@robinleehatcher.com

ABOUT THE AUTHOR

Author Robin Lee Hatcher, winner of the Christy Award for Excellence in Christian Fiction and the RITA Award for Best Inspirational Romance, has written over thirty-five contemporary and historical novels and novellas. There are more than 5 million copies of her novels in print, and she has been published in fourteen countries. Her first hardcover release, *The Forgiving Hour,* was optioned for film in 1999. Robin is a past president/CEO of Romance Writers of America, a professional writers organization with over eight thousand members worldwide. In recognition of her efforts on behalf of literacy, Laubach Literacy International named the Robin Award in her honor.

Robin and her husband, Jerry, live in Boise, Idaho, where they are active in their church and Robin leads a women's Bible study. Thanks to two grown daughters, Robin is now a grandmother of four ("an extremely young grandmother," she hastens to add). She enjoys travel, the theater, golf, and relaxing in the beautiful Idaho mountains. She and Jerry share their home with Delilah the Persian cat, Tiko the Shetland sheepdog, and Misty the Border collie.

Robin welcomes letters written to her at P.O. Box 4722, Boise, ID 83711-4722 or through her Web site at www.robinleehatcher.com.

$\mathcal{A}$N INTERVIEW
WITH ROBIN LEE HATCHER

What inspired you to write *Beyond the Shadows*?
As often happens with me, I envisioned the opening scene first. In my mind, I saw Deborah at the graveside with the gray sky behind her. I heard her voice distinctly telling me her story as the scene unfolded. It was so real to me, and I couldn't get it on paper fast enough.

What came a little more slowly was the realization that the central conflict of the book would be alcoholism. I can't say I was thrilled about that. But as God began speaking to my heart, I knew this was what He wanted from me.

Because my life has been impacted by the alcoholism of another, I know firsthand how ill-equipped most people are to deal with it, especially when it strikes in the family of believers. My experience tells me that very few Christians understand how prevalent this problem is within the church; it isn't simply a problem for those on the outside.

How much of your personal experience is found in Deborah's character?
In telling Deborah's story, I relied heavily on my personal experience and my own private struggles, both spiritual and emotional. I also talked to many friends and acquaintances who have been impacted by an alcoholic spouse, parent, child, sibling, etc. While our personal stories vary widely, they are hauntingly similar, too. And so it was for Deborah. Her experience in *Beyond the Shadows* was unique, and yet it was quite similar to mine and that of others.

Why is Gideon portrayed as a gentle, nonviolent alcoholic in the story?
Because that's what was true in my own situation. When I first began to suspect my loved one had a problem, I went into immediate denial. After all, alcoholics were unemployed and reeked of booze. My loved

one had a job and I never observed the drinking or smelled alcohol on the person's breath. I certainly never, through all the years, saw violent behavior. In fact, the opposite was true. My loved one completely withdrew from me, from others, and from life.

How did the Christians in your life respond as your situation became known?

Not always with love and compassion, I'm sorry to say. Yet I can understand, because I didn't always act with love and compassion myself. There were times I wanted to run away and not deal with it any longer, and there were some Christians who counseled me to do exactly that. But deep in my heart, even at the worst of times, I knew that nothing enters my life that isn't first filtered through the fingers of my loving God. So I tried to obey Him rather than following the wisdom of this world.

What is your greatest fear and how do you handle it?

My loved one is in recovery, and I suppose my secret fear is that the drinking could begin again. But fear is the opposite of faith, and part of my own recovery is to keep faith in action. It's a sin for children of God not to trust Him with every aspect of our lives. So I try to always choose faith and reject fear.

For most people impacted by the alcoholism of another, the need for control becomes a driving force and it causes them to behave irrationally at times. Accepting that they didn't cause the alcoholism— nor can they control either it or the alcoholic—is an important step toward finding peace in their own hearts. God is in control, and I try to remember that when fear presses in.

What hope can you offer readers who find themselves in a similar situation?

Rather than going into denial, get educated. Learn all you can about alcoholism. There are many books available, including some written by Christians who understand the importance of relying on the God of the Bible to help us deal with this—or any other—problem. In my opinion, the most helpful book I've read on the topic of alcoholism (and I've read more than two dozen) is *God Is for the Alcoholic* by Jerry Dunn (Moody Press, revised and expanded version published in 1986).

Don't go into hiding. Shame is a common feeling among family members. Those who love an alcoholic often withdraw into a world of silence and secrets. That's the wrong place to be. Refuse to isolate.

Get involved in a recovery program yourself, whether or not your loved one does. Alcoholism is a family illness. It impacts everyone it touches. Celebrate Recovery is a Christian recovery program based on the Beatitudes. (Visit www.celebraterecovery.com for more information.) Al-Anon, while not a Christian program, can be very beneficial for family members. (Visit www.al-anon.alateen.org for more information.) If you can't find a program on your own, contact Christian counselors in your area to see if they can recommend a good program for you.

Most important of all, *pray*. Pray for your loved one and pray for your own needs. Pray the Bible and let God's Word go deep into your heart. Seek God's will more than your own desires. Find godly people who will stand in the gap for you when you're too weak to pray for yourself. And when you reach the end of your rope and your hope, start praying all over again.

Finally, remember that God loves you. He's a God of miracles. He keeps track of all your sorrows. He's collected all of your tears in a bottle. He's recorded each one in His book (Psalm 56:8). No matter how dark the shadows may seem, there is light in Him. He really will not waste your hurt.

Plans

"For I know the plans I have for you," says the Lord. "They are plans for good and not for disaster, to give you a future and a hope."

JEREMIAH 29:11

1. What were Deborah's plans for her life? What circumstances caused her plans to change?

2. How did Deborah try to hang on to her plans? What mechanism did she use to hide her fears?

3. What were Gideon's plans? How did God fit into them?

4. What excuses did Gideon use to justify the changes in his plans?

5. What plans have you made, and how does God fit into them?

6. What excuses do you use to hang on to the past or ignore the present? How have you tried to control those around you?

Promises

"In those days when you pray, I will listen. If you look for Me in earnest you will find Me when you seek Me. I will be found by you," says the Lord.

JEREMIAH 29:12-13

1. What do these verses promise? What are the conditions?

2. Compare Deborah and Gideon in light of these verses. How are they alike? How are they different?

3. What drove Deborah to seek God? At what point did she begin to earnestly seek to live in the light of God's Word rather than in the shadows of fear and self?

4. How did other Christians help Deborah and Gideon to earnestly seek the Lord? What were some of the immediate changes? What changes took time?

5. Do you earnestly seek God in all that you do? What changes need to be made in your life in order to come out of the shadows of fear and self? How has God changed you?

Prayers

God is light and there is no darkness in Him at all.
So we are lying if we say we have fellowship
with God but go on living in spiritual darkness.
We are not living in the truth. But if we are living in
the light of God's presence, just as Christ is, then we have
fellowship with each other, and the blood of Jesus,
His Son, cleanses us from every sin.

1 JOHN 1:5-7

1. What do we learn about God's character from this passage? What does He offer us? What are the conditions?

2. Here is a suggested prayer from all the verses to offer back to God. Or take a few moments to write out your own response to these verses.

Lord, help me desire to walk in Your light and not linger in the shadows of fear and disobedience. Help me not to defend my excuses and fears for ignoring You and Your Word. May I long for Your plans and choose to trust in who You are and what You have done for me instead of myself. I confess that my fears, excuses, and controlling behavior are sins; they miss the mark— the plans You have for me. Thank You, Jesus, that You died for me and have cleansed me from every sin. I choose faith over fear, Your plans over mine. I choose to live in Your light and not to linger in the shadows.

May God bless you as you uncover the fear and shadows in your life. May you release them in faith to Him and walk in His light.

Visit us at tyndalefiction.com

Check out the latest information on your

favorite fiction authors and upcoming new

books! While you're there, don't forget to

register to receive *Fiction First,* our e-newsletter

that will keep you up to date on all of

Tyndale's Fiction.